To Seb

Happy C

from

December, 2019

GOALS for GOLD!

by
DAVID ALRIC

A tale of footballing magic and mayhem

GOALS for GOLD!

by
DAVID ALRIC

A tale of footballing magic and mayhem

Illustrated by Sue Boland

Acme Press

First published in 2016
by Acme Press Limited
c/o WSM, Connect House, 133–137 Alexandra Road, Wimbledon, London, SW19 7JY
dallison@acmepress.co.uk

Printed and bound in the UK by CPI Group (UK) Ltd, Croydon CR0 4YY

British Library Cataloguing in Publication Data. A catalogue record for this book is
available from the British Library.

ISBN 978-0-9568356-5-9

To Catherine, Helen and Richard

Acknowledgements

The author wishes to thank his wife, children and grandchildren for their help and patient support during the writing of this book; Pauline and Catherine for their secretarial and editorial contributions; Laura Penycate and Mr. Mesourouni for their footballing advice; Sue Boland for her wonderful illustrations and John Nicholson for his expert assistance in producing and publishing the final article. He would also like to express his gratitude to the Chessington World of Adventures Resort for their kind permission to include a visit to their theme park in the story

Contents

Preface

The first three books in this series, *The Promised One, The Valley of the Ancients* and *African Pursuit* form a trilogy which tells the extraordinary adventures of the Bonaventure and Sharp families in the jungles of South America and the African Congo. For those readers who have not read these books a brief synopsis of them is included below as a prologue. This story continues the series but it is neither a prequel nor a sequel to the other books. It is set at the end of *African Pursuit* just before the epilogue that completes that story. I suppose this book might therefore be called an 'interquel' and the trilogy has now become a tetralogy.

This tale is about football and, as in the other books in the series, I have tried to create an adventure story which combines an exciting fantasy element with a great deal of factual and educational material. It is written in a style that is fairly demanding in its use of grammar and vocabulary and to help the young reader with the latter I have included an glossary of any difficult or unusual words that appear in the text. An annexe to the story contains a detailed conversation between Christopher and the extraordinary visitor to his garden. This seems too long to sit comfortably in the main text but might, I hope, be of interest to some readers. Another annexe is the *'Animal and Elven lexicon'* in which I explain some of the neologisms used in the story. The reader may have some fun trying to guess the meaning of these before looking up the answers. In *'Notes on the names in the book'* I have explained the origins of the names used in the tale in the hope the reader will find these both amusing and instructive.

Folklore is an inexact science and descriptions of the nature, appearance and behaviour of the various magical entities that occupy home, field, forest and water vary widely across different traditions and cultures. As it is impossible to say which of these many descriptions are 'correct' or 'incorrect' I simply have endeavoured in this story to stray not too far from some of the more commonly accepted versions of the nature of these wonderful creatures.

I do hope you enjoy reading this tale of footballing magic as much as I have enjoyed writing it!

David Alric,
London, 2016

Prologue

This tale is the true – well, almost true – story of how two young brothers, Henry and Christopher, learned how to become brilliant footballers at St Luigi's primary school. But first you need to know a little bit about the extraordinary previous adventures of their elder brother Ben and their cousins, Clare, Lucy, Grace and Sarah.

Family Tree

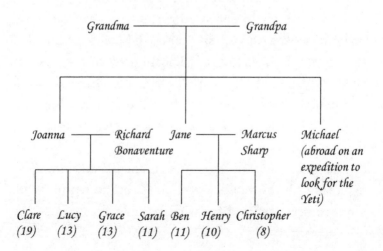

You may have already read the books in which I have described these adventures but, just in case you have not, I will give you a brief summary of them here.

The first book in the series, *The Promised One*, tells how Lucy Bonaventure bumps her head in a road accident which results in her being able to talk to animals. She discovers that she is 'The Promised One', a person the animals have been expecting for untold generations to come and restore harmony between human beings and the natural world. They will do anything she asks of them. Using this power she overcomes a gang of villains who have kidnapped her and rescues her father, Richard, a missing explorer who is trapped in a remote pre-historic crater in the Amazon jungle. This crater contains animals which existed over ten thousand years ago in the Pleistocene epoch and have now become extinct elsewhere.

The second book in the series, *The Valley of the Ancients*, is also set in the Amazon and tells how Clare, Lucy's elder sister, helps Lucy to defeat criminals who have stolen the secret of making invisibility robes and are determined to destroy the Bonaventures. They are operating in a secret valley which is the source of a rare ore essential to the manufacture of the robes but which also contains dinosaurs from the Cretaceous period, over sixty-five million years ago.

The story tells of the girls' dramatic adventures in exploring an incredible lost world of dinosaurs while engaged in mortal combat with invisible villains.

The third book in the series, *African Pursuit*, tells how

Sarah and Ben are kidnapped by poachers while on safari in East Africa and how Clare and Lucy use their animal allies to trail the poachers through Central Africa into the vast Congo rainforest where they rescue Sarah and Ben. In the depths of the rainforest Lucy discovers her twin sister, Grace, who was believed to have died as a baby when her parents, Richard and Joanna, had to flee from the Congo during a civil war. Grace shares Lucy's extraordinary power over animals and is revered by the creatures of the rainforest.

In order to protect Lucy and Grace from publicity and exploitation the Bonaventure and Sharp families think that the girls' ability to communicate with animals should remain a family secret so they have decided not to tell Henry and Christopher, the youngest family members, about their cousins' unique power until they are older.

1

Some Sinister Spectators

Henry and Christopher Sharp were bouncing on the edge of their seats with excitement. It was the final of a national under-elevens seven-a-side football competition in early May and they sat with their parents in a giant London stadium watching their elder brother Ben playing for St Luigi's, their school team. A storm which had threatened to drench both players and spectators had passed off to the east and now, as if to herald some dramatic event, the stadium was suddenly bathed in brilliant sunshine and a rainbow appeared in the sky.

The score was two all and there was just one minute to go to the final whistle!

Ingots Preparatory School had led from the start with a goal in the first minute, and a second goal just before half-time seemed to have sealed St Luigi's fate. They had rallied, however, with a goal early in the second half, and now, with only moments to go before the final whistle, an own goal by Ingots had brought the teams level. Ben, St Luigi's centre midfield, had played a great game, setting up their first goal with a brilliant pass to their striker and repeatedly blocking attacks from the Ingots' forwards. The Ingots' keeper now took a goal kick which their top striker tried to capture and failed, deflecting it to Ben. Ben surged forward to a storm of encouragement from the St Luigi's spectators, bypassed two Ingots players and found himself in the Ingots' midfield facing two defenders and the keeper. The referee looked at his watch.

'Come on, Ben, do something!' shouted his father. 'Nothing to lose!' And Henry and Christopher shouted:

'Shoot! Shoot!'

As Ben moved forward to set up a kick with his right foot, the ball hit a clod of earth and shifted to his left. The referee looked at his watch again and fumbled for his whistle. The crowd were now hysterical as the defenders closed in.

Ben gathered all his strength and shot with his left foot. The ball hurtled between the defenders, rising and curving towards the top right-hand corner of the goal.

Their keeper leapt and just managed to deflect the ball up to the crossbar with his fingertips. It bounced down and for a breathless moment seemed to hang in mid-air. Then it hit the ground just inside the goal line and rolled to the back of the net even as the final whistle blew. The St Luigi's supporters were ecstatic and poured on to the field. Soon Ben was surrounded by people thumping him on the back, hugging him and shaking his hand. The entire scene was like a junior version of the Cup Final and soon the players were swapping shirts and shaking hands. Ben

'Ben gathered all his strength and shot with his left foot...'

flushed with pride as the head teacher, Mr Jupiter, came onto the field and congratulated him.

On the touchline, stood Oskar Zdradzacski, known to all as Mr Z (or 'Z-man' by the pupils, behind his back). He was St Luigi's coach and senior PE teacher. Through his incredible hard work and teaching talent he had brought St Luigi's steadily up the junior league in the last few years and after the school had been runners-up in the previous year this victory was his crowning achievement. He was standing next to his opposite number from IPS and the latter now graciously turned and shook Mr Z's hand.

'Well done, Oskar, you've done a brilliant job with that team and you deserved to win.'

'Thanks, Tom,' Oskar replied, 'and we both know you were really unlucky with that own goal.' They laughed and shook hands again. Then Oskar nodded to the far corner, his face becoming serious.

'Who's that spooky-looking guy?' he asked. 'He's not with us so I presume he's with you.' Tom followed his gaze. A tall man stood at the far corner of the field. He had dark glasses and a trilby hat pulled down to one side so as partially to conceal his face. He and his two bulky companions, also in dark glasses, had arrived during the first half in a long black limousine car with darkened glass windows. They had watched the game impassively from their corner and had not tried to speak to any of the parents or other supporters. As Tom shielded his eyes from the sun with his hand to peer more intently the man caught his gaze, then turned abruptly and made his way back to the limousine with his companions.

'He does look vaguely familiar,' he said, 'but I can't place him – he's certainly not one of our regular parents. Maybe he's a talent spotter – it seems you can't start with the kids too young nowadays. Your Ben Sharp could soon be getting an offer he can't refuse!' They both smiled and then made their way over to talk to their respective teams, pushing their way through the excited crowd of parents and relatives still surrounding them. They would have been excited and intrigued to know that after leaving the stadium the limousine went straight back to one of the most famous football clubs in the world.

That evening the Sharp family went to Ben's favourite Italian restaurant, Al Burno, for a celebration meal. The conversation, inevitably, was about the day's exciting match. Henry and Christopher had been thrilled to see Ben emerge as the hero of the match and were discussing what would happen next season after Ben and his team mates went off to secondary school.

'I really hope I'll get into the first team,' said Henry, who was in the school year behind Ben, so would be in Year 6 after the summer holidays.

'Of course you will,' said Christopher loyally, 'and I want to get into the Year 4 team if I can.'

'Well you're both good players,' said Ben encouragingly. 'With any luck you'll both be in the teams you want. And I want to get into a team at my new school so let's all practise hard together in the garden during the holidays.

'There's a problem, though,' said Henry. 'Z-man doesn't like me and he picks the teams. He says he asks the other teachers what they think, but I know it's really him that decides.'

'But you're one of the best players in your year,' said Ben. 'You and Dominic and the Gormless twins. He'll need you in the team if he wants St Luigi's to do well again next year. Anyway,' he continued, 'he didn't like me much either but I did get into the team and today ...' he paused, embarrassed, not wishing to boast.

'... and today you showed him just what you're made of,' said his mother proudly. 'And Ben's right,' she continued, turning to Henry and Christopher, 'I know Mr Z, seems to come down a bit hard on the Sharp family, but you should all practise hard during the holidays and see what happens next term.'

Later that evening, when the boys were in bed, Jane and Marcus discussed the events of the day.

'Henry has his heart set on getting into the first team next year,' said Jane. 'I just hope he does – I don't think I can take the aggro if he doesn't.'

'Well, from what Ben said, he should, shouldn't he?' her husband calmly replied.

'I think so, but what Henry said at dinner was true. Mr Z does seem to have it in for all our boys. Even Christopher says he seems to pick on him more than the other boys. And I think I know why.' Marcus looked surprised.

'Why?'

'Well I know Mr Z is a great PE teacher and all that but I don't think he's very bright. I think he resents the fact that our boys are creative and musical and interested in so many things other than just football.' Marcus laughed.

'Trust you to have an explanation that makes him stupid and our lot perfect! They're probably all just over-reacting to his teaching style – and don't like being told to improve when they're doing something badly.'

'Maybe,' said Jane, doubtfully. 'I just hope that now Ben's leaving Mr Z will be nicer to Henry and Christopher – but I'm not holding my breath.'

'Well there's no point in worrying about things that haven't yet happened and anything could change. For all we know Mr Z might even have left the school by next term. Let's just wait and see. I expect everything will turn out OK.'

And on that optimistic note they went to bed, not knowing just how wrong Marcus was going to be!

The next day Obama Podpilasky sat in his office at the club thinking about the under-elevens final he had watched yesterday *incognito* with his burly minders. Everything he had seen made him confident that his plan was a good one. In addition to the famous club he now owned Podpilasky also ran several gambling organisations in various countries. He had observed that many gamblers preferred football to horse racing or other forms of gambling because they felt that they actually knew something about the game and were able to rate their favourite team's chances against various opponents. In other words, the average gambler felt that he or she was more likely to win a football bet than a bet on most other things. Based upon this observation Podpilasky, with his prodigious fortune, had bought the famous football club in which he now sat with the intention of manipulating the outcome of games in the Premier League so as to make even greater sums of money in his gambling empire. He had soon come to realize, however, that fixing the outcome of games in professional football in England was nowhere near as easy as it was in many other countries. Not only was there a high standard of professional pride and ethics in most clubs, but the scrutiny of players at this level in the game was so intense that the slightest suspicion of anyone attempting to 'throw' a game immediately aroused comment on social media and in the press, and from the highly knowledgeable radio and TV sports commentators.

It was actually his loyal assistant and economic advisor Alan Lackey who had hit upon the brilliant idea. He had suggested that instead of trying to fix matches in the Premier League, they should set up betting systems on *school* matches and fix them instead. They would be safe because the notion that anybody would or could deliberately arrange the outcome of football matches in a primary school league was too preposterous for anyone to take seriously. Finding a competent PE teacher in a primary school who was potentially vulnerable to blackmail had taken some time and effort, but with unlimited funds had not been too difficult, and Oskar Zdradzacski at St Luigi's primary school had seemed to be the perfect choice. Seeing the man lead his school team to victory yesterday had left Podpilasky in no doubt that they had picked the right man for the job he had in mind. He pressed a button on his desk and his PA immediately came through on the intercom.

'Yes, sir?'

'Send Alan up please, Pauline. It's about yesterday's school match.'

'Yes sir.'

Alan Lackey sat in his office checking the company accounts. His boss owned several companies around the world and for each Alan had two sets of accounts – one legal, for the scrutiny of tax and revenue officials in the various countries in which they operated, and one secret and illegal which generated millions of pounds through various nefarious means, ranging from drug and shady arms deals to extortion rackets and illegal gambling activities. A buzzer sounded on his desk and his PA came through on the intercom.

'Mr P wants to see you Mr Lackey – it's about school football.' She didn't say when – she didn't need to. If Podpilasky asked to see you he wanted to see you immediately. Lackey got up and took the lift to the penthouse floor where Podpilasky's luxurious office suite was located. The door to his private office was open and Podpilasky nodded and waved his cigar for Lackey to sit down in one of the deep leather armchairs. He said nothing until a uniformed manservant had put a silver tray of coffee and chocolate biscuits between the two men, bowed and left the room quietly, closing the door behind him.

'Good morning, Alan, how are the accounts?'

'Good morning, Obie,' Alan replied – he was one of the few people on the planet allowed to address Podpilasky by his nickname. 'The accounts, as always, are booming.'

'Good, and as a result of your excellent idea I think they are going to boom even more.' He paused and sipped his coffee before continuing. 'As you know, I went along to the schools final yesterday. I saw Zdradzacski in action and I'm certain he's our man. You did a great job in finding him.' Alan acknowledged the compliment with a nod and a smile but said nothing – Podpilasky didn't like interruptions. 'I think it's time we met up with him for a little chat. As you know I'm going abroad for the next two months but there's no hurry. We can't do anything until the start of the next football season. I'll leave you to fix up a meeting with Zdradzacski during the summer holidays.' Lackey returned to his office, asked his PA to arrange a private luncheon room for three in his favourite restaurant in early August, then sat down to draft an invitation to Oskar Zdradzacski at St Luigi's Primary School.

2

A Plot is Hatched

On the last day of the summer term Oskar received an invitation to lunch at a posh restaurant in London, The Holly. The invitation, delivered to the school by hand, was signed simply as being from "a well-wisher". Oskar was consumed wth curiosity and accepted the invitation. Once inside the restaurant, he found himself escorted by the staff to a small private dining room with oak-panelling and crystal chandeliers. There, sitting behind a table laid for three with beautiful glassware, napery and cutlery were two men, one of whom Oskar instantly recognised as being the manager of one of the most famous football clubs in the country. Even though the man was sitting Oskar could see he was very tall – even taller than he had previously realised. He was dressed in an immaculate light-grey suit with a perfectly knotted silk tie and matching silk handkerchief in his top pocket. He was familiar to Oskar through the numerous television interviews and sports documentaries in which he regularly appeared, but with his carefully groomed iron-grey hair, finely-chiselled features and piercing blue eyes he was in real life at close quarters even more distinguished and handsome than Oskar had appreciated. A gold tiepin studded with diamonds, a signet ring and gold cufflinks adorned with some heraldic embellishments in precious stones suggesting family links to some east European dynasty, completed the picture of arrogant affluence.

He did not get up as Oskar came in but the other man did. He was of medium height, bespectacled, bearded and balding. There was a black leather briefcase on the floor propped up against his chair.

'Hello,' he said, shaking Oskar's hand. 'Mr Zdradzacski I presume?' Oskar just nodded, his mouth was too dry to speak and his heart was beginning to pound. The man's grip was confident and powerful and Oskar suddenly realized his own palm was slightly damp with sweat. What on earth was this about? 'Please sit down,' the man continued. 'I am Alan Lackey and, as you probably know, this –,' he indicated to the seated manager, '– is Mr Obama Podpilasky.' Podpilasky nodded politely to Oskar but didn't attempt to shake hands. 'I am one of Mr Podpilasky's private financial advisors,' Lackey continued, and I have nothing to do with the football club, you understand.' Oskar nodded again. 'First of all, can I ask if you will give us your word that this meeting and anything said here will remain confidential. I mean – ' he paused briefly for emphasis, '– *completely* confidential irrespective of whether or not you decide to, er, co-operate with our plan.' For the first time Oskar detected a hint of steel beneath the man's courteous exterior.

'Of course,' said Oskar, eventually finding his voice. There seemed nothing to lose by agreeing to this curious request.

'Thank you,' said Lackey, 'and now let us enjoy our meal before we get down to business.' He pressed a bell and a waiter appeared within a few seconds to serve them a magnificent lunch. During lunch they talked of, course, about football, and Oskar was surprised and flattered by how much they knew about his own career and of St. Luigi's achievements. They made it clear that they considered him already to have become something of a legend in the world of primary school football. After lunch, over coffee and brandy and cigars Mr Podpilasky leaned forward and fixed Oskar with his cold blue eyes.

'And now, Oskar, I have a proposal to make.' He paused and drew on his cigar. He spoke almost flawless English and Oskar remembered that he had bought the club after making a fortune, some thought mostly by illegal deals, in his native country, which was either Russia or a neighbouring east European country; he couldn't remember the exact details. 'I have an only son, Ivan, and I have recently remarried. Ivan, unfortunately, doesn't always see eye to eye with his stepmother and he misses his mother. She, sadly, passed away five years ago in a tragic accident.' Oskar vaguely remembered the case and seemed to recall that her death had been regarded by some as being under suspicious circumstances. He said nothing and clearly Podpilasky didn't expect him to.

'Ivan is the apple of my eye, as I think the English say, and he attends Ingots Preparatory School.' Oskar nodded – he knew the school well: they were St Luigi's principal rivals and in May had been runners-up in a national under-elevens final. 'Now my boy is clever, of course,' said Podpilasky, 'but he is not very good when it comes to exams – they don't suit his personality – and his place in class, despite my generous contributions to school funds and the staff pension schemes, suggests that his talents are not yet fully appreciated by the teachers. He is, however, very good at football and while I hope and indeed expect that one day his business talents will emerge and he can take my place in the numerous commercial activities I undertake, I want to ensure that he enjoys a career in top-class professional football. This is where you come in, my friend.' As he paused to sip his brandy Oskar summoned up the courage to speak.

'What do you want me to do – give him some private tuition?'

'Ah no', Podpilasky said with a smile, 'he already receives that and under a small – ahem – financial arrangement I have with the PE teacher at Ingots, he is now the chief striker in the Ingots team.

'Do you have a photo?' asked Oskar. Podpilasky wasn't used to being interrupted and a flicker of disapproval crossed his face. He remembered that he wanted this man on side though, and gave a charming smile.

'Of course!' he said, and taking his mobile from his pocket flicked his finger over the screen and passed it to Oskar.

'Yes, I thought so,' he said after scrutinising the display. 'I've seen him play on several occasions. He's a fantastic player.' It was true, he was a very good player thought Oskar, but it was certainly helping his football progress to have this man as his father. 'So how *can* I help?' he continued.

'This is where it gets a little ... interesting, shall we say. The first thing is that my boy is desperate for Ingots to win a schools league next year. He knows that the talent scouts from my club and other clubs watch the schools' leagues with great interest. The earlier they can identify boys with talent, the sooner they can focus on training them to join the junior sections of their clubs. Now I, of course, do have some influence over my talent scouts, but to avoid accusations of nepotism it would greatly help if Ivan was the chief striker in the best primary school team in the country.

'So ...?' said Oskar. He began to sense what was coming with a mixture of apprehension and excitement.

'So, as you run one of the consistently best teams in the league I want you to make sure that Ingots win next year. This you will do by ensuring your team beats other rival teams, so as to diminish their placings in the league table, then losing all your matches drawn against Ingots.' He sat back, drew on his cigar and gazed steadily at Oskar. There was a long, long silence broken eventually by Oskar.

'If ... just let's say *if* I agreed to this ... ' Podpilasky said nothing but stared and waited. 'If I agreed, how could I be sure of winning all the matches I would need to win?' Podpilasky smiled: he knew already that he had hooked his fish.

'Well, as it happens, there's somebody I'd like you to meet.' He nodded to Lackey, who spoke into his mobile. A few seconds later a door concealed in the panelled wall swung open, and an enormous man entered. His massive chest was bursting out of an ill-fitting suit and the sleeves of the jacket were stretched tautly around his bulging biceps. His neck was more suited to an ox than a man and was the same width as his shaved head. His bull-like appearance was enhanced by a gold ring in his left nostril.

'Oskar,' said Podpilasky, 'I'd like to introduce you to my colleague Ron Pollard.'

Ron advanced and shook Oskar's hand. Oskar was a large, fit man but his hand felt like a child's as it disappeared into the vice-like grip of this formidable specimen of humanity.

'Ron is one of my most valued assistants,' continued Podpilasky. 'He leads a dedicated team of ... of professional experts. Ron will contact you in due course and offer any assistance you may require in your footballing arrangements.' He turned and nodded curtly to Ron who left the room.

'What – what kind of arrangements?' asked Oskar, not entirely sure he wanted to hear the answer.

' A very good question,' said Podpilasky. 'Well, I'll be a little more specific. Let's say you have a key match against – what's that school that was third in the league this year?'

'Hope Preparatory,' said Oskar.

'That's it, Hope,' said Podpilasky. 'Now let's say you're playing Hope. Am I right in thinking it might greatly

'Ron is one of my most valued assistants...'

improve your chances of winning if say, their best striker were to be mugged on the way to the match and lose his sports bag with his favourite boots in?'

'Yes, of course,' said Oskar.

'And if it were a really vital match one might need to be a little more imaginative. Say the striker's family were driving to the match and the car wouldn't start on the day because the fuel pump seemed to have disappeared during the night – or the car started but the brakes failed because of a fracture in the master cylinder. Or take the goalkeeper. Say the Hope goalkeeper was cycling to school the week before the match and got hit by a white van; nothing too drastic but, say, a broken arm or a broken leg. Do you get my drift?' Oskar certainly did.

'But – but how ...?' his voice tailed off.

'Ah, that's where Ron comes in. You just notify him of any special arrangements you need before a match and leave it up to him. He's extremely reliable, if a bit over-enthusiastic at times.' He paused for thought.

'There's just one thing. He was very close to his younger brother, Ken. Ken worked with a mining company in the Amazon jungle and about two years ago he was killed in a tragic accident. He was trying to save his companions who were being attacked by some maniac – and his *daughter*, can you believe, in the middle of the jungle – when they blew him up with some mining explosive. He was something of a hero because he was killed while trying to protect his companions. Anyway, Ron was devastated by his loss and since then has been a bit ... well, he gets easily upset. I'm just telling you so that you don't start arguing with him, especially about his plans for doing one of your jobs. He's fine if you just let him get on with it – OK?' Oskar nodded. It was certainly OK with him. He did not have the slightest intention of disagreeing with Ron Pollard about anything.

'And God help that pair who killed his brother if Ron ever finds them. I wouldn't be in their shoes for a million pounds,' continued Podpilasky. Nor, Oskar thought to himself, would I.

'Now there are two things I haven't yet mentioned', said Podpilasky. 'The first, I know, you'll be very interested in. If you agree to help me you will be putting yourself to some considerable trouble and inconvenience and, as Alan here will tell you' – he glanced at Lackey who nodded vigorously in agreement – 'I am an extremely generous man to those who assist me. For undertaking this little task I shall set up a safe deposit box in a Swiss bank. Into that account I shall pay one Krugerrand* every time your team succeeds in fulfilling the instructions you will be given by Alan. You will also receive one thousand pounds in cash which will be delivered to your home. On the day Ingots wins the league you will receive an additional five Krugerrands and five thousand pounds in cash and our arrangement will either terminate or continue for another year if we both wish it to do so. Oh, and as you will have to drive to all these matches you'll need a car. One will be parked in the drive of your house tomorrow, the keys will be in the exhaust pipe and all the documentation confirming

*Author's note: A Krugerrand is a gold coin. Please see glossary for further details.

you are the owner, together with road tax and insurance will be in the glove compartment.' Oskar gulped. This was the best thing that had ever happened to him. He wondered what kind of car it would be. 'So, do we have a deal?' Oskar pulled himself back from an imaginary drive under the channel to a top hotel in Paris next weekend.

'Er, yes. Definitely. Thank you!'

'Good.' Podpilasky stood up and offered his hand to shake on the deal. He held onto Oskar's hand after the shake and squeezed it a little harder as he continued. 'There's just the other thing I was going to tell you. About the confidentiality I mentioned earlier. I know you are a gentleman and a trustworthy professional and you wouldn't dream of mentioning any of this to anyone. Am I correct, Oskar?'

'Yes, of course,' Oskar croaked, wondering when he could rescue his hand.

'But I always take out a little ... let's call it *insurance* ... in these matters which I thought I should share with you.' He relinquished Oskar's hand, sat down again and nodded to Lackey who opened his briefcase and slid a faded newspaper article across the table between their glasses.

Oskar picked it up and turned white. The paper trembled in his clammy hands. There, in a ten-year-old newspaper article from his native country in Eastern Europe, was his picture above an article describing his conviction and prison sentence for defrauding the sports stadium in which he had worked. He had bought brand-new sports equipment and sportswear and secretly exchanged it for grossly inferior equipment with a dealer who had then sold the quality goods on the black market at almost full price. The dealer and Oskar had shared the profits on the scam. On release from prison Oskar had paid the same dealer to arrange a false passport for him and had started a new life in England with glowing, but completely false, references. As he actually was a very good PE teacher he had done well at St Luigi's and his future career – until this moment – had seemed secure. He fought to try and remain casual and gave a weak smile.

'Well, in the light of all you've said I think I'd like to help. But ...' as he paused Podpilasky smiled and nodded encouragingly for him to continue. '... but, there are practical issues. I believe I am a good teacher and I know I've got a good team. But you – of all people – know that football can be a chancy business. What if I do my best, take your generous payment, and still fail to get Ingots to win the league? I can see that we can nobble other teams using Ron and his team, but how can I ensure that my *own* team will win or lose to order?'

'That's your problem but what I would suggest from our experience with adult teams is that you bribe or threaten the two or three of your best players to do what you want.' He paused for thought. 'Oh, one final thing. My son is a little unpredictable and may sometimes want an unusual score result in some of your matches, but Alan here will keep you informed on a regular basis.' Oskar thought this seemed a little odd but said nothing. They were paying him so much they could ask for whatever they wanted.

'Well, I think that's it, don't you?' said Podpilasky. The interview was clearly at an end and Lackey rose and went to the door. Oskar got up and pushed in his chair.

'Thank you very much – and I think you're a fantastic father to do all this for Ivan.'

He walked unsteadily to the door which Lackey opened for him and closed quietly after him.

After Oskar had gone Lackey turned back to Podpilasky.

'Quite a touching remark that last one,' he said, and they both laughed.

'Do you think he suspects anything?' Podpilasky asked, when the mirth had subsided.

'I think he thinks the whole thing does seem very elaborate just to satisfy a boy's whim,' Lackey replied, 'but he appreciates that you need to give the boy a chance to make it in first-class football and he thinks he is simply benefiting from the indulgence of someone who has got more money than he knows what to do with. If you're asking whether he knows what we're really up to I think the answer is no!' Podpilasky nodded.

'I agree, he doesn't suspect the gambling scam and he's definitely the right man for the job …' he paused, then added ominously, '… but if there's the slightest hint of duplicity on his part … well, Ron may just have to put in a little overtime …'

That evening Oskar looked up Krugerrand on the internet. He found it was an investment coin containing pure gold, just one of which, to his astonishment and delight, was worth over a thousand pounds. This – in addition to the cash he had also been promised – was serious money and he was more determined than ever to do everything Podpilasky had requested. He left the computer, sat down and thought long and hard about his plans. If, using Ron, he could nobble key players on an opposing side, Luigi's could win any match – so that was not a problem. The problem was how to *lose* a match when that was required. Ideally he would need to persuade his two best strikers, a defender and the goalkeeper to cheat. He thought about the seven or eight candidates for next year's team. The keeper was excellent, but was a very serious and honest boy who couldn't be persuaded to do any such thing. There were three players who were far and away the best in the school: the Gormless brothers and Henry Sharp. Henry Sharp came from a close-knit family whose parents were involved and interested in all his school activities, academic as well as sporting. It was unthinkable that he would collude in anything underhand. That left the other two strikers, the Gormless twins. Now they were a different kettle of fish. Their father had never been seen at the school and it was rumoured that he was in jail. Their mother struggled to cope with two younger children, and the twins were getting out of control. When she came to pick up the twins after school with a pushchair and a toddler she looked careworn and frazzled and rarely spoke to the other parents. The twins were disruptive at school and bullied other children. Their academic performance was abysmal and their homework, if done at all, was always poor and late. They had twice been caught in petty thieving from other pupils or staff but the head teacher had been reluctant to report this to the police because he and the staff did not want to place further stress on their long-suffering mother.

The one thing that was beyond dispute, however, was the fact that the twins were outstandingly good at football. They were just what Oskar needed but he knew their compliance wasn't enough. Henry Sharp was the problem. He knew that he could never fix matches when Henry was in the team. He was transparently upright and honest and his family, whom he would certainly tell, would be shocked beyond belief – and furthermore probably report him. No, Henry was going to have to fail the team selection process. But how? Henry was potentially the best player in the school and it would be extremely difficult to pass him over in the selection process. He sat drinking beer and lighting one cigarette from another, deep in thought. There was only one solution he decided, risky though it was. He needed the help of the Gormless twins in making Henry look much worse than he really was, by never passing to him, trying to injure him, mocking his ability and generally demoralising him. He decided that one of his first jobs next term would be to have a little chat with the Gormless twins. In the meantime, if he wasn't in a dream, his new car should be delivered tomorrow ...

3

Concussion and Conspiracy

Six weeks later it was late afternoon on a Thursday, the first day of the autumn term at St Luigi's and the final lessons of the day were in progress. Oskar, who had a free period, had finished for the day and was sitting in his swivel chair with his feet on his cluttered desk smoking a cigarette. Smoking was banned in the school but he kept a packet in the sports locker next to his desk and had a cigarette during most of his free periods when Len Hutton and Stanley Matthews, the other sports teachers with whom he shared the office, were not there. In the small village where he had lived as a boy virtually everyone had smoked including both his parents, all unaware of the risks, and he had started almost without thinking. Now, in a completely different culture, he had realised he should give up the habit but had never quite got round to doing so. As usual he had opened a window and switched a fan on to disperse the smoke. Len and Stan knew he smoked of course, the room smelt permanently of smoke and they found the occasional cigarette butt in the steel wastepaper bin but, for the sake of a peaceful life, said nothing. From where he sat Oskar could see the staff car park and he gazed out proudly at his gleaming new car. It had already become a topic of feverish discussion in the school, universally admired by the pupils and producing a range of reactions among the staff varying from assumed disinterest to outright envy. He had debated long and hard with himself as to whether to bring it to school. He knew it would arouse speculation as to how he could afford it on a teacher's salary but pride had won the day and he had driven it into the school with a roar of exhaust and squealing of brakes on the first day of term. He had simply told the teacher most interested in gossip, in complete confidence, that a rich and eccentric uncle had died in Australia leaving him some money. The uncle, a motoring enthusiast, had specified in his will that the money should be spent on a sports car of Oskar's choosing. The lie had spread around the school within hours as Oskar had known it would and that little problem had been overcome. His next job was to talk to the Gormless twins. He hadn't seen them today but decided he would have to look them out tomorrow – he had to speak to them before the term's football programme got properly started. The bell went for the end of school and he got up and threw his cigarette out of the window into the flowerbed. A few moments later Len came in.

'Did you hear about Christopher Sharp? he said.

'No, what?'

'Poor kid banged his head on a goalpost during a lunch-time practice. Got knocked out. Stan went to hospital with him in the ambulance. He's just texted to say they've done a scan and he seems OK now but they're keeping him in overnight', He looked at his watch. 'Sorry, must dash. See you tomorrow.' Oskar said goodnight and decided to go home himself. Little did he suspect that Christopher Sharp's accident was destined not only to frustrate his wicked footballing plans but to change his entire life and the lives of countless others.

The next day he was in his office during the lunch hour when he saw the Gormless twins admiring his sleek new car. It was just the opportunity he had been waiting for and he sauntered outside and greeted them.

'Hi boys. Good holiday?'

'Fantastic car, sir.' He was the only teacher in the school that they addressed with any respect.

'Yes, it's great fun to drive – only trouble is, there aren't any roads in England on which I'm allowed to take her up to a decent speed. She's barely ticking over at 70.' They all laughed. 'Now,' he continued, 'I've been having a few thoughts about football during the holidays. How would you guys like to make some extra pocket money? A *lot* of extra pocket money. It would have to be secret though, *really* secret. It would be sort of ... breaking the rules a bit.' Their reaction left him in no doubt that he had picked the co-conspirators he required. 'Look, there's quite a lot of the lunch break left. Why don't we go to my office and

'Fantastic car, sir.'

have a little chat ? I think I saw some chocolate biscuits on Mr Hutton's desk and he's not back till later.'

Half an hour later, just before the bell for afternoon school, the twins left Oskar's office with barely concealed smirks on their faces. They had long been split into different classes at the universal request of those who taught them and, as they rounded the corner to go to their separate classrooms, they high-fived each other.

Left alone, with a free period ahead of him, Oskar made a coffee and sat thinking about the recent discussion. It had gone well. The twins were already jealous of Henry: they couldn't deny he was their equal at football but they envied his family situation. There was a stark comparison between his loving and stable family situation and their own and they mocked but secretly envied his academic ability – he was consistently near the top of his class.

They had eagerly agreed to collude with Oskar in diminishing Henry's apparent ability and in occasionally making sure that St Luigi's lost a crucial match in the schools' league. Oskar had explained that they would still aim to be second or third in the championship and they were more than happy to forgo winning the competition in return for the generous 'disappointment consolation bonuses' that Oskar promised to pay each time they threw a match.

Oskar had planned team selection matches for all the year groups a fortnight after the start of the autumn term and he and the twins now had to make sure that in the next two weeks they completely demoralised Henry Sharp.

He smiled, lit a cigarette and cast another satisfied glance at the gleaming car parked outside: things were going rather well.

That same day, while Oskar was revealing his plans to the twins, Jane was at the hospital talking to a young doctor about Christopher.

'He's fine to go home now,' said the doctor. 'The tests have shown no sign of a fracture or any internal damage ...' he paused, and Jane suddenly felt apprehensive, '... but there is just one thing. The head scan shows that his pineal gland – that's a pea-sized structure in the middle of the brain – looks a bit larger than usual. I don't think it's anything to worry about but I want him to see a specialist just to be sure. I'll try and fix an appointment as soon as possible. Oh, and no school and definitely no football for ten days!'

And so, the following Thursday morning, after almost a week of worry, Jane and Christopher found themselves sitting in Professor Furrowhead's consulting room as he looked at Christopher's scan with Dr Pixel, the radiologist. The professor, who was a neurosurgeon, had already examined Christopher and now, after a few minutes of pointing and discussion with his colleague, he turned to Jane.

'I'm sorry you've had a worrying time over this, Mrs Sharp, but the scan is slightly unusual and the doctor who saw you last week was quite right to send you to me. Anyway, I'm certain that this is nothing to worry about and doesn't need any further investigation.' Jane's heart was pounding but now she felt a flood of relief at his words. 'I think Christopher's gland is simply at the large end of the normal spectrum,' he continued. 'In fact, I saw one quite similar to this in a girl of eleven a couple of years ago. She's perfectly all right, by the way. So you can go home and forget all about it. And you,' he turned to Christopher with a smile as he ushered them out, 'had better try heading the ball instead of the goalpost in future.'

Jane wanted to ask more about the girl but knew that the doctor was busy and in any case couldn't talk about another patient, so she thanked him and took Christopher home, feeling as though a weight had been lifted from her shoulders.

As soon as they got back she called Joanna Bonaventure, her sister, who had four girls and lived nearby After telling her the good news about Christopher she asked:

'Do you remember the name of the surgeon who operated on Lucy after her accident? I was wondering if it was the same man who saw Christopher today.' Joanna laughed.

'Are you kidding? I'll remember his name for the rest of my life. He's called Furrowhead – John Furrowhead. Is that who you saw?'

'Yes, said Jane. I ...' she was going to ask another question but decided it could wait. 'I mean, thanks. It's reassuring to know Christopher has seen someone so good.'

As they starting discussing arrangements for the week ahead Christopher interrupted and asked if he could go in the garden. 'Yes, but no football, no trampoline and no climbing frame until the weekend – you heard what the doctor said!'

Later that same afternoon at school the sun was shining down on the regular Thursday afternoon football practice. They were playing seven-a-side, and four forwards stood facing each other in the centre of the field, waiting for the starting whistle. On one side, in red bibs, were Wayne Gormless, the ball at his feet, and Dominic Goodman; on the other in blue bibs, were Henry Sharp, his red hair flaming in the September sun, and Darren Gormless, Wayne's twin brother. The Gormless twins were tall and stocky, Dominic was tall and thin and Henry was short and wiry. They were probably the four best players in the school.

It had been a terrible footballing start to the term for Henry. In the two games he had played so far since coming back to school he had performed badly. At least he *appeared* to have performed badly. The Gormless twins seemed to have gone out of their way to make sure Henry never got a decent pass and they had consistently fouled him on the few occasions he did get the ball. Mr Z seemed oblivious to their behaviour and had repeatedly and unfairly criticised Henry whenever possible.

A week on Saturday, only ten days away, all the school would be playing in trial matches and these matches would be used to select the first and second teams for each year group. The first team in Year 6, Henry's year, would represent St Luigi's, the current champions, in the national under-eleven premier league.

Today's match was one of the few practice matches left before the team selection match and Henry was desperate to do well and reverse the bad impression he seemed to have made since the start of term.

As bad luck would have it Mr Z was the referee. Though there were three teachers running the football, Henry noticed that Mr Z always seemed to happen to be the referee for his games.

As the starting whistle blew Darren stepped backward a pace and slipped behind Henry. Wayne passed the ball to Henry's friend Dominic, playing against him on the red team, and as Henry started to move to tackle him he felt Darren's foot in front of his. Darren pushed him forward with both hands so he tripped and fell heavily, Wayne had moved forward and as Henry fell towards him he brought his knee up into Henry's face. The pain was excruciating and Henry fell into the mud, blood dripping from his nose.

'Stay out of my way next time, carrothead,' snarled Wayne and as Henry started to get up he kicked him savagely in the ribs as he ran past him, knocking him back to the ground. He high-fived Darren as they both ran back to the ball in the blue midfield.

'At least his face matches his stupid hair now,' said Darren. 'Nice one!'

'Well it was a good trip you did,' said Wayne graciously. 'I can't take all the credit.' They both laughed.

The pain was so intense Henry couldn't stop the tears coming to his eyes and as he fought to regain his breath

'Stay out of my way next time, carrothead...'

sobs of rage and frustration wracked his body. He lifted his head and looked for the referee. As usual, Mr Z had pretended not to see the disgraceful fouls. He just shouted across the field.

'Stop snivelling, Henry Sharp, and get back up: you're losing the match for the blues again!'

As Henry struggled to his feet his side was intensely painful and he wondered if the kick had broken some ribs. He was determined not to cry in front of the Gormless twins and wiped his eyes and bloody nose with his muddy sleeve. As he did so the game swept back past him and Wayne kicked him in the back of the knee, causing him to fall again.

'I said keep out of my way, you little red scumbag,' he hissed as he ran on.

Dominic stopped and helped him up.

'You OK, Hens? Those stupid idiots have really got it in for you today – and Z-man hasn't once ...'

Stop chattering, you two!' Mr Z shouted. 'In case you hadn't noticed, some of us are trying to play a game of football!'

Henry stumbled back to his position. Thankfully his nose had almost stopped bleeding but his side was so sore that he did his best to avoid any further physical contact with the other team and knew that he had played a terrible game. Eventually the final whistle blew and Henry trudged painfully across to the school gate with Dominic whose Mum was going to take Henry home in case Jane had been held up at the hospital. His face was encrusted in dried blood and mud, his side was aching and he was furious and bewildered by what was going on. He knew he was a good player and he felt that Mr Z was being grossly unfair to him. The teacher had always made it obvious that he did not like Henry but, as a first-class PE teacher – the best the school had ever had – he had recognised Henry's footballing potential and had coached him to the best of his ability. He was desperate to maintain the high standard of football he had created in the school and simply could not afford to ignore somebody with Henry's talent. To that extent he and Henry had evolved a grudging respect for each other but this term Henry was aware that their relationship had seriously deteriorated. He had been appalled at how, since the start of the new term, Mr Z seemed to have intensified his favouritism of the Gormless twins and become almost vicious in his treatment of Henry.

At home Jane called Christopher in from the garden.

'I've planned a nice tea as you've had a strange day,' she said. 'Henry should be here soon, Dominic's Mum's dropping him off after football – I just pray he's had a good session today, he seems to have had some bad luck so far this term.' Just then the doorbell rang. Jane opened the door and was horrified to see the state Henry was in. She waved to Dominic's mother in her car and then hugged him.

'What on earth have they been doing to you, darling? You look as if you've been in a battle, not a football match.'

'Those rotten idiots, the Gormless twins kept fouling me,' said Henry. 'And Z-man, as usual, kept looking the other way. He's being really nasty to me this term. I'm never going to get selected a week on Saturday and I really hate him.'

'Well go and have a nice hot bath and when you come down your favourite tea will be ready. I just happen to have some frankfurters in the fridge and this seems a good time to get them out.' To her great relief Henry's grimy, bloodstained face broke into a little grin.

'Thanks Mum! I'll be down soon.'

Ben had texted to say he had a detention, so Henry and Christopher started tea as soon as Henry reappeared. Henry was calmer now and he told Christopher exactly had happened during the practice.

'Well I'm sorry Z-man's being so horrid,' said Christopher, 'but it's bad for me too. I've not been allowed to play at all since my accident and I'll only have next week to practice before the selection matches.'

Jane tried to comfort them both but there wasn't really much she could say to help them with their football problems. She was surprised at how solemn and thoughtful Christopher was – she hadn't realised how worried he had been about missing his football practice because of his accident. In fact, Christopher was worrying about something entirely different. Something quite amazing that had happened to him in the garden that afternoon. Something that was going to change all their lives.

4

Curious Goings-on for Christopher

Earlier that day, while Henry was still at school and Jane was chatting to Joanna on the phone, Christopher had wandered down the garden. At first it had been fun being off school but now he was rather bored on his own and wished his brothers were home. They had a very large garden and down at the end he wondered if he could kick a football about without his mother seeing him. He retrieved the ball from the flower bed where Henry had kicked it the previous evening and put it into the goal mouth of their white plastic goal. Just looking and planning a kick could do no harm, he thought. Then a movement caught his eye and near the shed he saw a cat playing with something. As he went over to look the cat ran away and on the ground he saw a mouse, which had cute little brown ears and seemed to be dead as it lay quite still on its side. Except it wasn't dead! As Christopher peered at it he could see its tiny chest moving rapidly with its breathing and there was no obvious sign of injury. He picked it up, marvelling at how light its tiny figure was, and gently stroked it.

'You're OK, now,' he breathed. 'I'll look after you.' Suddenly the mouse revived and scrabbled back onto its feet. It looked intently at Christopher with its bright little eyes then leapt from his hand to the ground and scurried beneath a nearby dock leaf. Christopher watched to see if it would run further away under the fence but it didn't and he sat down on a nearby log and waited.

'Christopher!' said a little bell-like voice. Christopher spun round but there was no-one to be seen. 'Christopher, look, I'm over here on the barrow.' Christopher looked over to the wheelbarrow and there, to his utter astonishment, stood a small figure. It was about twenty centimetres tall with pointed ears, pink cheeks, bright green eyes, an upturned nose and a merry grin. Most bizarrely of all, it was dressed in the strip of Christopher's favourite Premier League football team complete with tiny, brand-new football boots. On its head, looking incongruous next to its football outfit, was a small green hat.

'Who ... what ...?' spluttered Christopher, rubbing his eyes in disbelief.

'Thank you for saving my life just now,' said the little creature.

'But I've never seen you before,' said Christopher.

'Ah yes, I forgot. I was a mouse when you saw me. We Littlefolk can turn ourselves into any creature if we wish.'

'But the mouse is still under that leaf,' said Christopher, pointing. He bent down and looked under the leaf. The mouse had gone. 'At least he was until you spoke – I've been watching all the time.'

'Thank you for saving my life just now.'

'Oh, that's something else you need to know. We can become invisible – at least to you Greatfolk. In fact, that's how we usually go around. I was just leaving when I reached the barrow and then thought I should thank you. In fact I *had* to thank you, for those are the rules.'

'Whose rules?'

'I'll tell you more of those later. But one of the rules says that because you saved my life I can grant you a wish – a wish that must come true.'

Suddenly Christopher realised that he must be imagining things because of the bump on his head. He had had a slight headache all week and something must be affecting his brain. He must go and tell his mother that all was not well, but even though he knew this creature was a figment of his imagination it seemed rude to just walk away.

'I'm sorry, but I'm not very well and I'm going in to see my Mum. Goodbye.' He got up and turned to leave when the creature turned back into a mouse, jumped from the barrow and ran over to Christopher. It climbed up his trousers and shirt in an instant and ran down to his hand.

'Well,' the creature said, 'now you can touch me again and see that I am real. Please sit down now and we can talk.' Christopher gingerly put out a finger and gently poked the mouse. It was warm and furry and ... real. He sat down in a daze of confusing thoughts. The mouse jumped down and turned back into the little creature again. He also sat down, on a smooth stone in the rockery near the edge of the lawn. He sat in silence, watching patiently as Christopher gathered his thoughts.

'What are you and why were you a mouse?' he said, eventually.

'Good question,' said the creature. 'I am what you would call an elf – sometimes we are mistaken for pixies but they mostly live far away where the sun goes to sleep.' he pointed to the west. 'They are indeed our cousins but they are smaller than we are and fly about a great deal – though not as fast or as well as we do. As for being a mouse – well, I must confess I was being rather mischievous. I actually live with some of my kin in an elfnook at the bottom of the garden of your greatkin. There are many primroses there, which is important to us.' Christopher was about to interrupt to ask what his greatkin were but then realised the elf must mean Grandma and Grandpa. 'I have seen you there many times,' the elf continued, 'and enjoy watching you play with your brothers and cousinkin. One day I followed you home here to see where you live and then I saw something interesting.' He pointed over the fence. 'The Greatfolk lady who lives over there started to scream and I when I flew over to see what was happening I saw a little mouse running away. The lady was very scared. Well the next time I came to your house to watch you playing I saw her come out to hang up her washing. I turned into a mouse and hid in her washing basket. She screamed and ran inside when she saw me. How my friends and I laughed and laughed. Then for at least two moons she made her husband or children hang out the washing. But a few days ago she started to do it herself once more and so today I thought I would entertain my friends again by running along the washing line as she was putting her pegs up. I had just turned myself into a mouse when the cat pounced on me and if you hadn't saved me ... I just don't like to think about it.'

'She told my Mum about you,' said Christopher laughing, 'and my Mum was a bit scared about putting our *own* washing out after that.' He paused and thought for a moment. 'But if you can do magic and stuff how did a cat manage to catch you – surely you could become invisible or, even better, turn into a dog?' The · smiled.

'You're a smart boy. But that wasn't really a cat – it was a goblin.'

'A goblin!' exclaimed Christopher. 'But why would a goblin turn into a cat?'

'Before I answer that you need to know a bit more about the Littlefolk,' said the elf. We elven folk – like the leprechauns and the pixies – like to live in small groups and we move about a great deal, unlike the sprites, brownies, dryads and fairies who like to stay in the same places, usually in the woods near ponds and streams – especially the sprites. The goblins also stay in the same places and they have lived in the same dens for thousands of your years. They cannot cross the sea, the Great Salt, as we call it, so all the places they live in this land are known to all the Littlefolk. Their homes are called gobblehides – caves or large burrows like old badger setts, and though they can eat anything they must have fresh meat every day. There are ten goblin gobblehides in the land, five in the west and four to the north and one here, near the great city.

It was here long before the great city and is in a wood on Wimbledon Common.'

'But why would a goblin turn into a cat?' persisted Christopher.

'Ah yes, sorry, I forgot that's what I was explaining,' said the elf. 'Well, the truth is that the gobblekin are nasty folk – always after us. They spend most of their time deep in the woods but now and then one roams about looking for one of us and tries to catch us. They catch other Littlefolk as well – mostly sprites or brownies, but not the fairies, they daren't touch them. Much too powerful. Why a fairy would turn a goblin into a garden gnome in an instant and that would be that – for ever. And they don't touch hobgoblins either,' he added. 'Too big, and though they say they are friendlier than goblins they can be really vicious when they get angry.'

'What happens if they catch you?' asked Christopher, not sure if he really wanted to know the answer.

'They take us back to their great Gobblehide on Wimbledon Common where they have a magic barrier which even we cannot pass, and we have to work as their slaves for a year and a day. For every one of us they catch they get a piece of gold from the Gobbleking. They don't often catch us though. Fortunately they can't fly and they're usually quite stupid – the one that caught me was very clever to think of turning himself into a cat.'

'But he wasn't trying to catch you, he was trying to kill you', said Christopher. 'Why was that?'

'The answer to that is a long one,' replied the elf, 'which I will tell you on another day. In fact it is a very troublesome story that is soon going to affect you Greatfolk.' He paused, as if considering whether to tell Christopher more now, but clearly decided against it and Christopher sensed it would be rude to press him. 'Anyway,' the elf continued, 'thank you again for what you did and, as I said, you can now have a wish – anything you want as long as it is in the Faerie Code. Don't decide now because once you have decided it is irrevocable; think about it carefully and tell me another day.'

'What's irrev ... irrevocal – and what's the Faerie Code?' asked Christopher.

'Irrevocable means once you've decided you can't change your mind. The code is the rules drawn up by the fairies long, long ago for how the Littlefolk are to behave towards the Greatfolk. If, say, for your wish you asked me to kill someone I could not do that.'

'Something I was wondering,' said Christopher, 'is why are primroses so important to you?'

'We elves – and many other Littlefolk – must eat special things in order to be able to become invisible. We must eat primroses, so our elfnooks are always somewhere near where these flowers grow.'

'But what about when the flowers aren't there? The plants don't have flowers all the time do they?'

'No, they don't', replied the elf, 'so when they flower we collect lots, dry them and keep them safe so we always have a supply. If we run out we can eat the leaves but they don't taste so nice and aren't so powerful.'

Christopher was fascinated. Dozens of questions formed in his mind but one thing dominated his thoughts.

'Why ...?' he paused. He hoped he wouldn't offend the elf. 'Why are you dressed in my favourite football club's kit?'

The elf gave a tinkling laugh.

'I don't know what a club is, but I can see it is very dear to you for this is how you are always dressed. You must tell me more about it later – but now your mother is going to call you to come in. Think about your wish and I'll see you again soon. Fare thee well.'

And with that he disappeared. Sure enough the very next moment his mother called him from the French windows to come in for tea. He turned and stumbled his way to the house, his mind in a complete turmoil. Why didn't the elf know what a club strip was, even when he was wearing one? How did he know he was called Christopher? Could he really make a wish that would come true? Was this an after-effect of his accident? Or was he just going mad?

Even while hearing about Henry's unfortunate football practice during tea his mind kept going back to the extraordinary events in the garden and he worried all evening about the elf. Had he really seen him or had the bump on the head affected his brain in some dreadful way? He thought about telling his mother but he didn't want to go back to hospital and have more tests and he knew that is what would happen. Anyway the elf seemed real. But maybe that is what happened when your brain went funny.

Should he tell Henry or Ben? Definitely not – they'd just laugh at him – especially if he told them about the elf being dressed in a club strip.

No, he'd just have to wait till tomorrow and see if anything else happened. And his headache *had* completely gone and he *did* feel much better so it was difficult to imagine he was getting worse.

The next day Christopher went straight out into the garden. He felt much more cheerful. It was a bright sunny day and during breakfast he had decided that yesterday's events must have been some kind of strange daydream. But he had to make sure. He peered behind the shed and there was no sign of the cat or the mouse. Then, looking round to make sure his mother wasn't there, he called softly into the bushes.

'Elf, elf – are you there?' He felt a complete idiot and looked around again. If Mummy or a neighbour heard him talking to elves ... He called once more and then with a sigh of relief he went to get the football. His ten-day ban wasn't up until the day after tomorrow but surely a bit of gentle dribbling couldn't do any harm.

As he started to kick the ball he heard a giggle. He spun round. Had one of his brothers been hiding and was now ready to tease him? Then he remembered, there was no Henry or Ben – they'd both gone to school. But there was another giggle and there, sitting cool as a cucumber on the shed roof was the elf – dressed once again in the full strip of Christopher's favourite club.

'Did you call?' he asked with an impish grin.

'Er – yes,' admitted Christopher.

That means you believe in me and that means you can see me. We only rarely ever show ourselves to the Greatfolk

50

but even if we try they cannot see us if they don't believe we exist.' Christopher thought about this. He had told himself that the elf was in a daydream, but now he realised that in his heart of hearts he did know that everything that had happened was real.

'Please call me Christopher. I don't feel like one of the Greatfolk even though I must seem like one to you.'

'Fine,' said the elf. 'Whatever you say.'

'I - I'd had a bump on the head and thought that I'd imagined you, but I suppose I *did* know you were real – and I'm glad 'cos its really cool.'

The elf looked pleased.

'And it's cool for me too. We're not normally allowed to talk to the Greatfolk unless something special has happened but you saved my life so that's OK.' He paused. 'I think it *was* your bump on the head that made you able to talk to me. I have seen you many, many times before but yesterday I knew instantly that you had changed and would be aware of me. I asked my elvensibs and they said that very, very occasionally over countless aeons of olden times, one of the Greatfolk could talk to the Elvenfolk – sometimes after a terrible bump on the head and sometimes after being struck by a thunderbolt – *lightning* I think you would say but ...'

'What's an elvensib?' Christopher interrupted.

'It's one of my closest relations. We don't have brothers or sisters like you Greatfolk – just elvensibs.'*

* *For readers interested in Christopher's entire conversation with the elf, in which he learns about elfin lives in more detail, please see the appendix. At the end of the appendix the elf has just told Christopher that he is called Aelfred after a great king who lived long ago.*

Christopher had only ever heard of one king called something like that.

'Do you mean Alfred the Great – the one who burnt the cakes?' The elf grinned.

'I don't know of any cakes but he must be the king I mean. Anyway, Aelfred is my proper name but my elvensibs usually call me Alfie.'

'Can I call you Alfie too?'

'I would be honoured.' To Christopher's amusement the elf gave an old-fashioned bow as he said this. 'And now to your wish.' he continued. 'You have had time to think. What can I do for you?'

'It's kind of you to ask, but I'm a bit worried about it being so *irreverent*,' said Christopher.

'Irrevocable!' laughed Alfie kindly. Christopher grinned.

'That's right – irrevocable. I knew it didn't sound quite right. Anyway, would it be rude if I thought about it a bit longer?'

'Of course not. In fact I'm very pleased that you recognise it's a very big decision. Let's talk about something else. What is this club uniform you wear?'

Christopher was delighted to talk about his favourite topic – football – and explained everything about football clubs, the football league and how it was enjoyed by people of all ages. The elf was fascinated to realise that Christopher's kit was related to the game he had seen the boys playing on countless occasions. He explained to Christopher that his elfsibs were also interested and was delighted when

Christopher suggested that he brought them along when they next spoke. He was about to ask more about the rules when Jane called from the back door.

'Come on, Christie. We've got to go to the shops or there's nothing for your lunch.'

'See you later Alfie – got to go.'

'Of, course,' said the elf with a little wave. Christopher waved back as he ran to the house, his brain buzzing with all that he had learnt.

That evening, Friday, Henry brought back a note from Christopher's new class teacher, who of course hadn't seen Christopher since the first day of term. She knew he was coming back on Monday and wanted him to do the class homework for the weekend which was to construct something of his own choosing – something small enough to bring into school and show the rest of the class the following week. That evening he rang Grandpa.

'Grandpa, are you busy tomorrow?' he asked.

'Why?' said Grandpa cautiously. He had been caught out by Christopher's grand plans on several previous occasions and was learning. Christopher, on the other hand, who was just as clever as Grandpa, knew that the answer 'why?' meant Grandpa was free – otherwise he would have said 'no'.

'Well, I've got to make something for homework and I was wondering if you could help me. I'd like to make a miniature football set.'

'What – like little goal posts with nets you mean?'

"Yes, can you help me – please!' Grandpa was already thinking about what he might have in his greenhouse and shed and garage.

'Yes, that sounds like fun,' he said. They discussed what time Christopher would come and then Grandpa went and found some suitable pieces of wood and some fine-mesh garden netting in his greenhouse. He was a keen gardener and DIY enthusiast and had all sorts of materials to make things with – as Christopher and his brothers knew very well.

The next day Grandpa showed Christopher some sketches he had made and they got to work. Christopher had used Grandpa's vice before and now he clamped the wooden plant supports Grandpa had got ready, measured them with a steel tape and sawed them to the right lengths for the goal posts and cross-bars. Then they prepared some more sticks to make the rear posts and bars to rest on the ground so the goals would be stable. Grandpa helped him to drill some holes and after rubbing everything smooth with sandpaper, they screwed and glued the pieces together. Finally they cut some netting and fixed it to the two wooden infrastructures. For the corner posts they used some shorter sticks. Then they painted everything white with some quick-drying paint. Finally, Christopher cut out some corner flags from coloured paper and kept these to stick these to the corner posts when they were dry. He couldn't believe how realistic it all looked at the end.

'You don't have a ball do you?' he asked Grandpa. Grandpa laughed.

'Anyone would think you were going to play a miniature game,' he said.

'That's exactly what I *am* going to do,' thought Christopher, but he just smiled.

'I just want the set to look perfect,' he said. First Grandpa found a table tennis ball but Christopher thought it was too light. Then, at the back of the Wendy House, he found the perfect ball – an old squash ball – a small rubber ball, heavier than a table-tennis ball but about the same size. Christopher was delighted. Grandpa promised to bring the whole set over the next day when the glue and paint were completely dry.

As soon as Grandpa had left the next day, and Christopher had proudly shown the results of his workmanship to Jane and Marcus, he rushed down to the end of the garden and called the elf. Then he remembered that the elf lived round at Grandma's house. He was just wondering whether to go back inside when the tiny figure appeared from behind the shed.

'How did you know I was here?' asked Christopher, relieved to see him. 'I thought you lived at Grandma's house.'

'Simple,' the elf replied with a grin. 'It's called magic! We can sense when you want us and fly over.'

'Aha!' said Christopher, smiling. 'I suppose it was a silly question.' He looked around. 'But where are the others?' he asked, a little disappointed not to see Alfie's elfsibs.

'They are all here,' said the elf, 'but we must stay invisible unless it's absolutely necessary, so you can't see them. They can see and hear you, though.'

'Good. Now I'm going to teach you how to play football.' He positioned the two goals at a suitable distance, stuck the corner flags in, and made some white lines with flour he had pinched from the kitchen. Then he produced the ball and explained the rules of the game to Alfie and his invisible clan. When he had finished Alfie himself became invisible and soon Christopher was sitting on the climbing frame watching the little ball whizzing to and fro and occasionally going into one or other of the goals. Every now and then a little voice asked about a rule or stratagem and Christopher did his best to help them. They were very intelligent and, of course, extremely agile and skilful and Christopher was fascinated to see the movements of the ball. The elves said they found it difficult to stop themselves flying but Christopher explained that it would spoil the game if they left the ground and they had to pretend they could only run and jump like humans and not use any magic in their play.

Christopher was very busy the next week as he had to catch up with the work he had missed while he was off sick, but he still practised hard at football whenever he could. He was disappointed with his performance at the Thursday afternoon practice matches but was even more upset to hear that Henry had once again had a bad time with Mr Z.

Over tea Jane asked Henry what had happened.

'It was Wayne and Darren again,' said Henry through a mouthful of fish fingers. 'They kept fouling me and tricking me and stupid Z-man just let them and then blamed me for mucking around.'

'He hates both of us,' said Christopher, trying to console him. 'it's not just you. He's got special favourites in my group as well, and says I'll be lucky to get into the year 4 team. I even heard him say to smarmy Dean Foster that it would be a miracle if I got selected.'

'He really shouldn't talk to the other boys about you,' said Jane. 'Or maybe you misheard him.' She tried to comfort them both but inwardly she was seething at how unfairly her boys were being treated. She sighed and gave them some more chips.

'All I know is that they're picking all the teams on Saturday and neither of us is going to get picked,' said Henry.

'Yeah, we're both just failures,' added Christopher gloomily.

Don't be silly,' said Jane. 'Of course you're not failures. Are you saying that every boy or girl not in one of the football teams is a failure? That means most of the children in the school are failures. And in any case we all know you both should be in one of the teams but you just don't get on with Mr Z.'

'Don't get on …!' Henry said scornfully, mimicking her voice. 'Get real, Mum! He hates us and he's the unfairest git I've ever met.' Jane knew it was pointless to say any more. She had done all she could to support them both and now everything depended on Saturday's trials. At least parents were allowed to watch, so she and Marcus could go and cheer them on. In the meantime, she decided, the best thing was to give them their favourite pudding and went off to make pancakes covered in golden syrup.

After tea Christopher went down the garden. Because of his busy week he hadn't seen Alfie for several days but now he had finally decided what he wanted from the elf.

'Long time, no see,' said Alfie, who was very proud of the catch phrases he had picked up during his long life – and some of which he used in the wrong places.

He had appeared shortly after Christopher had called him and was sitting on an upturned flower pot in his club strip.

'Yes,' said Christopher, I'm sorry, 'I've been very busy with school and football and music and cubs this week.'

'Cubs? Whose cubs?' asked Alfie. Christopher laughed.

'Not *real* cubs – it's just the name of a group I go to where we learn things and have lots of fun. Anyway, I wanted to see you because I have made up my mind about my wish ...' He suddenly frowned and said in a worried voice '... it's not too late is it?'

'Oh no,' Alfie reassured him, 'it's never too late.'

'Am – am I allowed to ask something for somebody else?' asked Christopher, somewhat hesitantly. The elf smiled.

'Of course!'

'You see my brother Henry is very good at football ...'

'I know; I've seen him many times,' interrupted Alfie.

'... well what you may *not* know is that a teacher at school and some other boys have been mean to him and hurt him, and they are trying to stop him getting into the school football team. For my wish I would like you to help him get into the team: could you do that?' The elf smiled again.

'Nothing could be easier.' Christopher gave a sigh of relief.

'Oh good – I suddenly realised that this is what I wanted more than anything else and then I was worried you'd say you couldn't do it for some reason.'

'If he has been treated unfairly we are allowed to put things right,' said Alfie, ' and my elfsibs and I will be happy to do this. When do we need to do something?'

'On Saturday – that's two days from now – we are all playing football matches and, depending on how we play, the teachers are going to put us into first and second teams for each school year.'

'I see,' said Alfie. He paused and looked thoughtful. 'So *you'll* be trying to get into a team as well as Henry?'

'Yes – but a different one. He'll be trying to get into the Year 6 team – and I'll be trying to get into the Year 4 team. But you'll easily see which his match is, so you'll know the right one to go to.' The elf gave a an enigmatic smile.

'I'm sure I will. Now just leave everything to me and don't worry.'

Two Amazing Matches!

Saturday was a beautiful September morning and Henry and Christopher were already dressed for football when Jane came down to make their breakfast. Ben was still asleep and would go round to Grandma later in the morning for his weekly Latin lesson. They didn't teach Latin at Ben's school but he was very interested in it and Grandma had been giving him lessons since he was eight.

After breakfast Jane and Marcus went to the school playing fields with the two boys who were in a state of nervous excitement. There were three PE teachers in all and, as bad luck would have it, Mr Z was once again the one going to referee Henry's trial match.

'I knew it,' exploded Henry as soon as he saw the allocations. 'I just *knew* it. I can tell you now this is going to be *awful*.' Then he glanced at his parents and put on a determined expression. 'But I'm still going to try my best.'

'And so am I,' said Christopher.

'Well, I'm proud of you both,' said Marcus. 'And you're right – you have to try even harder if you feel the system is stacked against you.'

Henry's match was starting first and the teams trooped on to the field. There were two forwards on each side with Henry and Dominic in blue bibs facing Wayne and Darren in red bibs.

'Don't let those idiots get us down,' Dominic muttered to Henry. 'Let's try and beat them.'

'OK,' said Henry,' but he knew in his heart of hearts they would be fouled and unfairly treated.

The starting whistle blew and, as Henry passed the ball to Dominic, Wayne launched a late and vicious tackle on him, kicking him in the ankle. Mr Z seemed not to notice. Darren meanwhile had pushed Dominic to one side and taken control of the ball. He dribbled it expertly down the field past the midfielders and the backs, feinted to one side to fool the keeper, and then scored. There was only muted clapping from the spectators, many of whom had seen the foul.

'Looks as if Henry's predictions are bang on,' said Marcus gloomily to Jane. She nodded and glanced at her watch. In a few minutes one of them would need to go to over to the other pitch where Christopher's game would be starting. She decided that she'd better be the one to go – she didn't think she could bear to watch much more of Henry's humiliation.

The whistle blew and the game restarted. Henry passed to Dominic who managed to kick the ball forward before being tripped by Darren. Henry ran past Wayne to face William and Dean, the red midfielders who were now in possession. William passed the ball to Dean as Henry moved towards them. In a curious change of direction, however, the ball suddenly stopped going towards Dean and curved round to Henry's feet. The incident happened so quickly that only the three boys saw what had really happened. Henry darted forward with the ball and moved expertly down towards the red goal. He passed to Dominic to bypass the red left back and Dominic passed it back to Henry before the right back could tackle him.

Now Henry faced only the red goalkeeper – Kevin, the biggest boy in their year – who came out swiftly to confront him. Just as Henry was about to try and dribble around him the ball moved away from his feet by a full metre to the left. The keeper moved aside to get the ball but as he did so the ball suddenly reversed direction and came back to Henry's feet. The goal was open in front of him and he made no mistake, smashing the ball into the back of the net.

'My goodness!' Jane heard another parent nearby exclaim. 'Did you see that? That red-haired boy is amazing – so quick I didn't really see how he did it but he left that keeper standing.'

There was a stunned silence around the entire pitch, both on and off the field. Then the blue team went wild and the blue supporters burst into spontaneous applause, shouting and clapping. Jane and Marcus hugged each other and shouted out congratulations to Henry. The man nearby now turned to Jane.

'Is that your lad – the ginger-haired genius?' Jane nodded proudly, tears in her eyes and her face split by an enthusiastic grin.

'Yes, that's my Henry.'

'Well I've never seen anything like that goal – not even in the Champions' league. Your boy seems to be able to control the ball even if he isn't touching it. He must put a special spin on it – it's incredible ... just incredible ...' His voice tailed off as the players gathered to restart the game. The eyes of every spectator were now on Henry. Wayne, his face seething with rage, muttered to Darren through clenched teeth.

'Let's fix the little dork.' Darren nodded.

The game restarted and instead of passing to Darren, Wayne kicked the ball back to William in midfield then moved towards Henry in a circling movement with Darren. It was a trick they had perfected through long practice. While all the spectators and the referee were watching the ball as it went back to midfield, Darren would seem to stumble into Henry by accident while Wayne elbowed him or kicked him.

But this time as Wayne moved forward Darren remained rooted to the spot. He jerked his leg and almost fell over. Henry seized his chance and ran outside him towards William.

'What the hell are you doing?' snarled Wayne. 'We could've had 'im then.'

Darren looked down and to his astonishment saw that his laces were tangled so tightly that he couldn't move either of his feet.

'My laces ...,' he stuttered, '... they're tangled.' He bent down to sort them out and as he did so there was another

'My laces...,'
he stuttered,'... they're tangled.'

roar from the spectators. William in the red midfield had taken the pass back from Wayne and was moving swiftly towards Henry. As he started to dodge round Henry, nudging the ball from his right foot to his left foot, the ball seemed to decide to move in exactly the opposite direction and ended up in Henry's possession. Henry moved swiftly past the astonished William who had no hope of retrieving the ball and Henry now faced the right back. Then something quite extraordinary happened that had the spectators delirious with excitement.

As Henry moved towards his opponent he touched the ball lightly to keep it in front of him but he must have done a very special touch, for the ball rose straight up in the air, seemed to hover for a second above the back's head and then fell gently down behind him. The back looked up in bewilderment but couldn't see the ball he wanted to head. In the meantime Henry ran round him, connected with the ball and shot immediately for goal from just outside the penalty area. He had to shoot quickly – the left back was almost upon him – so the ball was only heading for the centre of the goal rather than to the side or the top, and the keeper put up his arms for what he knew would be an easy save. At the last moment, however, the ball swerved abruptly beyond his reach and ended up in the left-hand corner of the net. In the whole of primary school football history there can never have been so much applause from so few spectators. They went wild and Jane and Marcus were literally jumping for joy as the blue team ran to hug Henry, now flushed with excitement as the red team stood in bewildered amazement at the way the match was going.

'Your boy is simply unbelievable,' said the parent next to Jane and Marcus. 'Did you see how he flicked the ball over that back – and then ... that goal! What kind of a spin can you put on a ball to make it go straight and then, at the last minute, turn in mid-air into a tight curve? I've never seen anything like it!' And from the animated conversation around the touchline it was plain that everybody felt the same. The parent turned to them again as the whistle blew for halftime.

'I think I should introduce myself – I'm Toby Clements – and Max is my son.' He pointed to the blue goalkeeper.

'I'm Jane Sharp and this is my husband Marcus,' said Jane. 'So you're Max's dad! We're so pleased to meet you. Henry often talks about Max – he says he's the best goalie in the school. 'He thinks ...' she hesitated but then carried on regardless, '... he thinks that Max is not ...' she hesitated again – but Toby interrupted:

'He thinks Max is not given the credit he deserves by Mr Z.'

'Exactly!' said Jane, relieved that Toby shared their thoughts about Mr Z. She was about to elaborate on the problems her own boys had experienced when she suddenly put her hand to her mouth in horror.

'Oh Heavens ...' she stared in alarm at Marcus. '... Christopher!' But Marcus had remembered at the same time and was already hurrying across the field to Christopher's match which was just about to start.

'Sorry,' Jane said to Toby, 'but our other boy, Christopher, is playing in the Year 4 match over there,' she pointed. 'But Marcus and I got so involved in this match ...'

'Not surprisingly!' interjected Toby. 'How could anyone possibly think about anything else during a display like that?'

The referee, his face black as thunder, who had spent most of halftime chatting with the red team, now blew his whistle for the second half.

This time the red team kicked off and Wayne made a straight, clean pass to Darren as they moved smoothly toward the blue forwards. Straight though the pass was, however, the ball mysteriously curved before reaching Darren and ended directly in front of Henry who made a long forward pass out to the right wing where Adam was moving up fast from midfield to take control of it. He skilfully outmanoeuvred the red midfield player marking him and then kicked a soaring pass inwards across the goal mouth. Henry jumped up to head it but the ball was high – too high – however, as his head came underneath the ball it made a downturn as if attracted to a magnet on Henry's forehead and then, after what only seemed the slightest touch by Henry, accelerated and curved into the top right-hand corner of the goal. The keeper didn't have a chance and once again the spectators were vocal in their support and praise for Henry's skill. In the final moments of the match Henry received a beautiful forward pass from Dominic and dribbled skilfully past the red midfield. The backs couldn't reach him in time and it was just Kevin the goalkeeper and Henry. Kevin came rapidly out towards Henry to reduce his scoring angle but Henry flicked the ball straight up into the air. Kevin inevitably looked up, only to see the ball gathering new momentum as if from some incredible spinning tactic (though it didn't appear to be spinning at all) and then hurtling into the far corner of the goal. Henry, who didn't know how it had happened, almost felt sorry for Kevin as he saw his expression – a mixture of rage and bewilderment – but then he remembered the many times he had belittled and insulted him and ganged up with Wayne and Darren to kick or injure him, unseen – and sometimes seen – by Mr Z.

Once again the spectators erupted in delight and several other parents came up to congratulate Jane on Henry's spectacular ball control.

The game eventually finished with the blues winning by seven goals to one, Henry having scored five and created the other two. Jane rushed over to Marcus to tell him the result. He hugged her in delight then turned back to the field.

'And you're just not going to believe what's been happening over here!' he said, pointing to where the forwards opposing Christopher were lining up to start again after a goal. 'We're already three nil and Christie scored all the goals. All that practice they've been putting in in the garden has certainly paid off. Their performances have been amazing.'

Back in the changing room Wayne and Darren sat next to each other on the mudstained bench taking their boots off. Both boys had been forced to admit that Henry had played a superb game and Wayne was beginning to think that maybe they had treated him rather unfairly in the past. He was still cross with the way Darren had stood still early in the match after he had given him a good pass and he had let Henry streak between them taking the ball with him. He glanced across the room to check that Henry wasn't listening but Henry seemed deep in conversation with Dominic.

'Talking about playing well,' he said cautiously, not wanting to offend his brother who had a notoriously short fuse, 'what made you stand still like a moron when we could've sorted Henry out?'

Darren looked embarrassed as he started to pull his trainers on. He paused for a while before speaking.

'I didn't know whether to tell you this,' he said slowly, 'but you know how my laces got ... got tangled?' Wayne nodded.

'Well, it sounds absolutely crazy, but they weren't just tangled.'

'Whaddyamean?' Wayne was intrigued but had the feeling that an over-elaborate excuse was on the way.

'They were tied together – in a neat knot. A funny knot like you see in pictures of sailors' knots or scouting knots.'

'But you'd already been playing for about ten minutes. Why did you tie your laces together in the middle of a match?'

'That's just it – I didn't. I just don't know how it happened.'

'Well nobody else came along and tied them up in the middle of a game, so they must've just got tangled into a knot. There's no other possible explanation.'

'No-o,' said Darren, 'I suppose there isn't. It just happened at a *dead* inconvenient time though – and probably cost us a goal.'

Just then Mr Z came over after having just spoken to Henry.

'What were you two playing at? The blues absolutely thrashed you.'

'I'm sorry,' muttered Wayne. 'We both seem to have had a bit of an "off" day.'

'Well, it happens to the best of us sometimes,' said Mr Z, just don't let it happen too often – and it hasn't helped me with my selections – the entire blue team actually did better than the entire red team today, even though most of the pupils I was likely to select were in the red ream. And as for Henry Sharp ...' he dropped his voice and glanced over to check that Henry wasn't listening '... either he's massively improved or he had a succession of amazing flukes. I'm going to have to think about this very carefully over the weekend.'

Later that afternoon the Sharp family went to a pizza restaurant for tea to celebrate the successes of the day and Ben could hardly keep up with the excited babbling of his brothers as they gave him a blow-by- blow account of their matches.

'Well it sounds as if they'll have to select you both for your teams,' he said when he could eventually get a word in edgeways. 'You both seem to have been the best on the field in your matches.' Henry's expression changed.

'I'm not so sure about that,' he said. 'Afterwards Z-man came over and said I'd done well with a few "lucky sequences" as he called them. "Lucky sequences!" And when he went over to talk to Wayne I heard something about an "off" day, and then when they looked over at me I heard Z-man saying something about a "fluky" game.'

'Well I agree with Ben,' said Marcus. Even if Wayne did have an off-day – which anyone can have – it still doesn't diminish your achievements and it's difficult to see how you can't be picked for the team.' Henry was pleased with everybody being so supportive but he still had his doubts. He really didn't trust Z-man an inch. And he was, of course, right.

Jane was a bit late picking the boys up from school on Monday and they were waiting at the school door as she hurried up the drive. Christopher looked animated but as soon as she saw Henry's face she knew things weren't right. As she drew near Christopher rushed up and hugged her. She saw Henry about to speak but shook her head and put her finger to her lips over Christopher's head.

'I'm in the team, Mummy,' said Christopher. 'I've been selected!'

'Well done!' said Jane. 'I'm really pleased for you.' And she gave him another hug and a kiss.

'But Henry ...' he started, but Jane interrupted.

'Let Henry tell me himself, love.' She turned to Henry. 'What's happened?'

'I knew they wouldn't pick me – I told you didn't I? I just *knew* it.'

'Who have they picked then?' Jane knew all the likely candidates. The school matches were seven-a-side so the team usually comprised nine or ten players, to allow for players sitting out on the bench, and one reserve.

'No one,' said Henry. 'They're having another trial on Wednesday after school can you believe it? Z-man said that as some of the boys were "a bit off-colour" on Saturday he was going to have another trial before choosing the team. But that's stupid 'cos the only boys who said they weren't playing well on Saturday were Wayne and Darren and I expect they're going to be in the team anyway. So it's just an excuse to try and keep me out. He's hoping I won't do so well on Wednesday. It's really, *really* unfair.' Jane could only agree. His logic was undeniable.

'Well it does seem unfair,' she said, 'but at least there's still a *chance* you'll get in – and I'm sure you'll be in the second team anyway.'

'I don't want to be in the second team,' said Henry savagely. 'I'd rather not be in any team. Anyway, I *should* be in the first team.'

'I know you should, said Jane, 'and I expect you will be. There's no reason why you shouldn't play just as well on Wednesday as you did at the weekend.'

'I'm not so sure about that,' said Henry. 'On Saturday I felt as if I couldn't do anything wrong. I've never had that feeling before. I just knew the ball would go where I wanted,' he paused. 'I know it sounds stupid,' he continued, 'but I felt as if the ball was going to the right place all on its own – sometimes I'm sure I barely touched it and it whizzed off just where I wanted it to go.'

'Well that's because you've been practising and have become better than you realize,' said Jane comfortingly. 'As I said before, there's no reason at all why you shouldn't be just as good on Wednesday.'

'Yeah,' said Christopher. 'Kevin's brother's in my class and he said you were great. And Kevin told him he didn't have a chance of stopping any of your goals.' Jane looked at him fondly for his loyal support and Henry was obviously cheered up by their comments.

'Thanks, guys. I'll just do my best and try and prove Z-man wrong.'

Christopher was in something of a quandary. He had meant well using his wish to help Henry, and now realised that he hadn't really believed his wish would make any difference. But the events of Saturday made it quite difficult to imagine the elves hadn't helped in some way. And that meant he couldn't tell Henry. First of all Henry probably wouldn't believe him and, worse, it he did, he would be upset that his success was because of magic and not because of his own ability. On the other hand, Christopher suddenly thought, he himself had also played brilliantly on Saturday, so maybe it was all the practice he and Henry had done and was nothing to do with the elf. Cheered up by this thought, he decided he would tell Henry about the elf – but not until after Wednesday, just in case it affected his game in some way.

Wednesday started off cloudy and overcast but the forecast was for a fine afternoon and evening. Only a few parents were able to watch the match on a Wednesday afternoon, but Jane and Christopher were there and Ben came to join them just in time. Mr Z had split the teams to form the boys into different groupings and Henry was now co-striker with Darren on the blue team, with Dominic and Wayne facing them on the red front line. The blues kicked off and Henry felt a reassuring thrill of power as soon as he touched the ball. He knew immediately that the ball was behaving as it had on Saturday. He pretended to pass to Darren at his right then nudged the ball forward outside Dominic while he ran inside Dominic opposite. The ball behaved even better than he had dared hope and curved back towards Henry behind Dominic. An onlooker in the air above them would have seen the ball and Henry perform a neat ellipse around Dominic. Henry got his toe under the ball as he continued forward and flicked it up. It soared neatly over the head of the midfielder ahead as Henry ran round him and collected the ball beyond. He was now at the edge of the box and kicked straight for goal. The ball curved to the right around the oncoming back and then as the keeper dived towards it curved *back* to the left, executing an S-shaped trajectory and passing over the spot from which the goalkeeper had just dived. It thumped into the back of the net to a stunned silence from the entire field. A few seconds later the blue team erupted in praise for Henry. As Jane clapped and shouted she glanced at Mr Z who on this occasion was not refereeing but observing from the touchline. He was standing open-mouthed in wonder at what he had just witnessed. Jane quickly looked away again in case he saw her staring and waved to Henry who was walking back, flushed with pleasure, to the middle of the field to face the red team kick-off. And so it went on. Again and again Henry outplayed his opponents and the eventual score was seven nil. As the final whistle blew Mr Z knew he was beaten. Forcing a smile (the effort made him look like a wolf with toothache) he came over to Jane.

'Henry did very well. We'll be sorting out the selections tonight but I thought you should know that I'll definitely be picking him for the first team. He'll be our main striker.'

Jane thanked him and explained that Ben and Christopher had been practising hard with him for weeks in the garden. Ben had rushed off to congratulate Henry but Jane couldn't resist telling Mr Z that he had already been selected for the first team at his new secondary school. Mr Z, only too aware of how unfair he had previously been to Ben, mumbled some congratulatory remark and then excused himself, apparently having suddenly remembered something he had to tell the teams before they left the field.

6

A Magical Football Practice

After Wednesday's trial match Oskar returned to his office deep in thought. The first three weeks of term had not gone smoothly. Despite Wayne and Darren having done their utmost to foul and injure Henry Sharp the boy had got better and bettter at football and his outstanding performance in today's match had made it impossible for Oskar not to include him in the team. As he sat chain-smoking and wondering how he was going to manage to satisfy Lackey's demands with Henry in the team, his mobile phone rang.

'Oskar?' It was Lackey on the line.

'Yes,' replied Oskar. 'Hello. I was just thinking about you.' This was true, but his thoughts had not been exactly what Lackey might have wanted them to be. Lackey wasted no time on any greeting.

'I'm calling about the first league match on Saturday.'

'Ah, yes,' said Oskar. 'I was expecting to hear from you.'

'Well Mr Podpilasky has been talking to Ivan. He says you are playing St Mediocre's on Saturday, is that correct?'

'Er, yes.'

'And Ivan says they are a rubbish team who will have no chance of winning the league, do you agree?'

'Definitely.'

'Good. In that case we don't want St Luigi's getting too far ahead on points at this stage so you will lose the match. Goodbye!' There was a click as he rang off.

Oskar stared in horror at his phone. Lose to St Mediocre's! It was unthinkable. But that, he reminded himself, was the whole point of his agreement. He was getting paid to do the unthinkable, but now as he faced the reality of the situation and what he had to do he felt himself breaking out in a cold sweat. Just then the door opened and his colleagues Len and Stan came in.

'Caught in the act!' said Len. Oskar felt a new shudder of fear – what had they overheard?

'It really is a filthy habit,' said Stan, grinning as he opened the window wider and fanned the smoke out with his notebook. 'Not really good form for the country's top primary sports teacher!'

Oskar felt a wave of relief sweep over him as he stubbed his cigarette out.

'I'm sorry ... I just need a cigarette after the excitement of the afternoon.'

'Wow,' said Len, 'Henry Sharp is just unbelievable. We'll be retaining the championship if this carries on.'

'Starting with a pathetically easy win on Saturday,' added Stan and they both laughed. Oskar didn't laugh; he just felt another cold sweat coming on. Neither of the others noticed.

Meanwhile, back in the Sharp's garden, Christopher was at that very moment talking to Alfie.

'Do you mind if I tell my brothers about you?' he asked. 'I feel a bit sneaky letting Henry think he's got so much better at football when it's really because of you and your elfsibs.

'Yes, I would like to meet them,' said the elf. 'It would be good to talk to Henry about football – he's already improving just through being more confident. But remember, I can hear what *they* say for I understand the Greatfolk tongue, but they can only hear what *I* say if you are present. You and I are communicating by our thoughts, mine in the elven tongue and yours in the Greatfolk tongue. They will only hear me through you.'

'But how?' asked Christopher.

'We have no idea,' said the elf with a little smile. 'That is why you are so special. Your brain can do things that others cannot.'

Straight after school on Friday, Christopher asked his brothers to come outside and play football. When they got to the end of the garden Christopher turned to the others.

'There's someone I want you both to meet,' he announced. Ben and Henry looked around, perplexed. The three of them seemed to be alone.

'OK Alfie,' called Christopher, and the elf suddenly materialised, sitting on an upturned flower pot and dressed as usual in his club kit.

'Hi Alfie!' said Christopher, enjoying his moment of showing his big brothers something about which they knew nothing. 'This is Ben, he's eleven and this is Henry, who's ten.' The boys stood still and stared in stupefied silence as the little creature flew up to each in turn and poked them on the nose with his tiny hand.

'Who ... what ... who are you?' spluttered Ben eventually.

'He's an elf and I saved his life 'cos he was pretending to be a mouse and got caught by a cat who wasn't really a cat but a goblin pretending to be a cat,' said Christopher in a rush. 'Oh, and I can speak to him because something happened to my brain when I bumped my head. Alfie says it's only happened to a few special people in the whole of history,' he added proudly.

'And why are you in that club strip?' asked Henry.

'Ah, I forgot,' said the elf in his tiny, tinkling voice. 'Silly me,' and in a twinkle he disappeared and reappeared in a different strip.

'Wow!' breathed Henry. This was the strip of his favourite team.

'Cool!' breathed Ben. Pleased with the effect he had created, Alfie turned to Ben and in another twinkle, his outfit transmogrified into Ben's favourite strip. Ben was delighted.

'*Seriously* cool!' he exclaimed, then thought for a few seconds. 'But if Christie's so special how come me and Henry can talk to you as well?'

'Henry and I!' corrected Henry, grinning. The elf also smiled, but turned to answer Ben.

'We Elvenfolk can understand your speech, though among ourselves we speak in the Ancient Tongue,' replied the elf. But you could not hear *me* speak if Christopher was not here. He receives my thoughts and ...' the elf struggled to explain his thoughts.

'I know,' said Ben. 'He's like a sort of transformer. He converts your thoughts into our speech. But ...' he frowned, '... I hear *you* saying things, not Christie.'

'It is a puzzle to me too,' said the elf. 'All I know is that when Christopher is here my thoughts can bounce off him and you can hear it as my speech. As I told your brother, this is a most unusual power which only few Greatfolk have had in all time past.'

'And how do you know about our football strips?' asked Henry who was getting bored by things nobody could understand.

'He's been watching us play for ages,' said Christopher, 'and knows what we all like to wear. I had to explain to him what the kits mean and now he understands all about the premier league. I've also taught him and his elfsibs to play football –' he added proudly, '– so he knows how to help us in real games.'

'What's an elfsib?' asked Ben.

'It's a sort of brother and sister rolled into one,' explained Christopher. 'The elves are like a giant family, all related, but without mums and dads. Oh –,' he added, '– and there aren't male or female elves but Alfie's got a boy's name so I think of him as a 'him.' The elf smiled and nodded, apparently satisfied with this explanation of elfin kinship. Henry, however, had seized upon the import of one of Christopher's previous remarks.

'What did you mean, *help us*?' he asked suspiciously.

'Ah, I was coming to that,' said Christopher hesitantly. He felt awkward about explaining it all to Henry but fortunately the elf decided to take over. His voice suddenly became soft and mellifluous and Christopher immediately sensed that some magic was in the air. As the little creature spoke he seemed to soothe Henry, who listened intently to what he said.

'Let me explain everything to all of you. When Christopher saved my life I gave him a wish – a wish that had to come true. But instead of asking for something for himself – a bike, or a new electronic gadget, or whatever – he asked that Henry should get into the school football team.' As Henry flushed with pleasure at hearing of Christopher's generosity the elf continued.

'Under the rules ...'

'What rules?' interrupted Ben

'I will explain,' replied the elf patiently. 'Everything we magic folk – fairies, goblins, sprites, pixies, leprechauns, brownies and all the others – everything we do to the Greatfolk is governed by an ancient faerie code. It stops us using our magic to interfere with human lives except in self-defence or a reward for a good deed. Under the rules, if a human asks for a wish that benefits another, we can confer an extra favour on that generous person. In your case, Christopher ...' the elf switched back into his usual club kit and turned to Christopher in one dazzlingly quick movement, '... I helped you get into *your* team as well as helping Henry get into *his*.' Christopher gaped in astonishment.

'So *that's* why you've both improved so much,' said Ben. 'The elves have been helping you!' Henry frowned.

'So I got selected on Wednesday just because you helped me?' he said to the elf.

'Certainly not: you *always* deserved to be in the team and I simply made sure that it happened.'

'But – but,' Henry hesitated. He didn't want to be rude. 'But isn't that kind of cheating. Helping us against the other boys without their knowledge?' The elf smiled.

'You are a fair and honest boy and I will answer your question. All magic is a kind of cheating if you think about it – it breaks the normal rules of nature – and we have to be very careful how we use it. I have been talking to my elfsibs, some of whom are very interested and knowledgeable about football and I have learnt many things. In your case both you and Christopher have been unfairly treated over a long period of time and I am putting that right. As you didn't know what was going on I had to help you by doing some magic tricks with the ball – it was rather fun; we elves have a reputation for being very mischievous after all. Now you both *know* you are being helped, my plan is that to start with we work together to overcome your opponents; then, as you gain in confidence and acquire the respect you really do deserve from other players – you are, after all, both really skilful footballers, my elfsibs and I will gradually do less and less so that once again you are completely on your own. If after that you still can't compete with the others then that is hard luck but how it must be.'

'At least you will have put them back on a level playing field,' said Ben, and they all laughed.

'Now,' said the elf, 'let's have a little practice at elven-assisted play. You go in goal Ben,' he pointed. 'You take the ball, Henry, and you, Christopher, stand between Henry and the goal and act as defender.' They all took up their positions as instructed.

'Now I am going to become invisible but remember, I am your fellow striker Henry.' As he spoke he disappeared into thin air but his voice continued. 'Now don't forget to pass to me Henry even though you can't see me.' Henry moved forward to Christopher, then hesitated. He looked at the empty grass. He couldn't believe it would work: surely the ball would just disappear into the flower bed.

'Pass! come on, pass!' shouted the elf's little voice. Henry passed the ball sideways to the left at the last moment. He then ran forward to the right of Christopher and magically the ball turned back towards him behind Christopher. He collected it and shot at goal. Ben moved to stop it but at the last moment the ball swerved past him and crossed the line.

'Wow!' they all chorused. 'Fantastic!' The elf reappeared and looked pleased at their reaction.

'But doesn't the ball hurt you?' asked Christopher. 'Especially if it's going fast, and how can you make it do what you want? It's so big and heavy for you. When I made the mini-football set with Grandpa we got you a small ball'

'Yes,' said the elf, 'and very useful that was too. When learning to play with that we didn't use any special powers so we could understand how the game felt for you Greatfolk. But now in real life we need to be able to manipulate the big ball that you use. To do that we use magic. Watch!' He walked over to the upturned flowerpot – an old fashioned heavy red earthenware pot. 'If I stand close to the pot my magic is very strong, look!' He flicked his hand and the pot lifted up, turned over and settled on to the ground. The boys were impressed. The pot was the same height as the elf and considerably heavier. 'So if I am close to an object, the elf went on, I can influence its position or direction without touching it. If I am too far away I cannot move it.'

'It's just like magnetism,' said Ben suddenly.

'I don't know what you mean,' said the elf, 'but I think you understand. So in one of your matches I always play with several elfsibs. One of us tries always to be near enough to the ball to change its direction and, of course, if it's in the air we fly alongside it.' They practised for a while and the three boys rapidly became skilful at using their invisible teammate.

'I realise now,' said Henry after a while, 'that in the two games I've played so far with you helping, you had to take the ball off me and then give it back to me – I couldn't really understand how the ball was doing that. But now I know you are there I can use you to much better effect. I'm really looking forward to the next game.'

'What about when we start playing other schools in the league – like tomorrow?' asked Christopher. 'I thought elves and fairies were meant to be good. Why should you be helping us to do something that isn't really fair on other people?'

'Well you don't know it,' said the elf, but your school has also been unfairly treated in the league – you won the championship last year but that was even more of an achievement than you realise. Some of the other schools were not behaving in a fair and proper way and need to be taught a lesson. Their PE teachers gave them goals they should not have had when they were refereeing and ignored fouls. They included children of the wrong age in teams – all sorts of bad things.'

'How do you know all that?' asked Ben.

'We Littlefolk know all kinds of things,' said the elf, 'and I have told you before that many of my elfsibs take a great interest in football. Just trust me when I say that any help I give you will be setting the record straight and once that is done I won't help any more.'

'Why don't you just go and put things straight without us?'

'Because that would be interfering in Greatfolk affairs without good reason. We are only allowed to help you because Christopher saved my life.'

'So if Henry doesn't play tomorrow you can't do anything in the match?'

'Correct.'

The next day was bright and sunny – perfect for the first matches of the under-eleven league. St Luigi's team appeared fit and eager, looking forward to an easy win in their home match against St Mediocre's – a team that had ended second from the bottom in last year's championship. Henry was disappointed to find that Z-man had put him on the bench for the first half; Wayne and Darren were both playing as forwards with Dominic and Adam in midfield. As Henry sat on the touchline watching Wayne strolling up to the centre line he was struck by Wayne's expression. Instead of his usual arrogant smirk he looked uncomfortable – odd, thought Henry, as he was about to start playing in a game that would end in a certain win for St Luigi's. Henry was right: Wayne was feeling uncomfortable. He didn't like losing but that was what he had to do. He comforted himself with the thought of the two crisp twenty pound notes Oskar had slipped into his hand the previous evening for him and Darren, and prepared to do his worst.

The whistle blew and Wayne passed clumsily to Darren who stumbled and missed the ball. The Mediocre's striker was through the gap and onto the ball immediately. Wayne turned back to chase him but seemed somehow only to get in Dominic's way as he moved to tackle the oncoming striker. A few seconds later St Mediocre's were leading one–nil. And so it went on. Henry turned to Ben and Christopher standing as spectators behind the bench.

'What *are* those idiots doing? It almost looks as if they're *trying* to give the ball away! And why aren't Elfie and his lot doing something?'

'They can't,' said Ben. 'Remember what he said yesterday – he can only help if you're playing!'

At half-time St. Mediocre's were leading four–one and Oskar decided their lead was sufficient to risk having Henry on the field: Len and Stan had both suggested this and he had no good reason for refusing them. He would replace Dominic in midfield with Henry, keep Wayne and Darren as forwards, and hope that they could exclude Henry as far as possible from the action.

The whistle blew and Wayne passed to Darren. As the ball moved across it swerved sharply back and ended at Henry's feet who was already moving forward to receive it. As the Mediocre's striker approached, to his utter amazement, Henry passed the ball to an apparently empty space on his left and then ran past him on the right. Safely behind the striker, Henry seemed mysteriously to become re-united with the ball and ran on towards the midfield. The centre midfield had observed what had happened with astonishment but wasn't going to let it happen to him. As Henry approached he moved to block the curious pass he had apparently used to out-manoeuvre the striker but Henry didn't pass to the invisible elf: he simply passed to Adam who stormed downfield, with Henry swiftly following and catching up. As the back came up to Adam he passed to Henry who then kicked a stunning goal into the top corner of the net – a goal he felt particularly pleased with as he could sense that the shot had been entirely his own. As the St Luigi's supporters cheered at this change in fortune Len turned to Oskar.

'Good move bringing on Henry, Oskar. If he carries on like this he may just have time to pull it off.' Stan agreed and they turned back to watch the match, so missing the murderous look with which Oskar greeted these words.

And so the match went on, with St Luigi's eventually winning seven–four.

As Henry left the field with his proud family he glanced across to a corner of the pitch where Oskar, his face purple with rage, was remonstrating with the Gormless twins.

'Look at Z-man,' he murmured to Ben. 'He's telling off his favourites for a change.'

'Well they did play pretty badly,' said Ben, 'they deserve it!'

On Monday Henry and Christopher had a good session at the after-school football club, despite Z-man being in a foul mood, and they walked to the gate looking happy, despite being tired and muddy. Grandpa was waiting for them as planned and they both greeted him with a hug. They were just walking towards the car when a long black car with darkened windows drove past them and in through the school gates.

'What have you all been up to?' Grandpa joked. 'Looks as if the Secret Service is coming to investigate.' Henry suddenly stopped.

'Oh gosh, I've forgotten my maths book and I need it for my homework! I can still get in the back way. You take Christie in the car, Grandpa, and I'll walk home – I'm allowed now I'm in year 6.' He thrust his bags into Grandpa's hands and ran back to the side door where Mr Yale the plump caretaker, known to all the boys as 'Chubby' behind his back, was talking to one of the cleaners. The limousine was now parked nearby and a uniformed chauffeur was polishing the black windows. Mr Yale recognised Henry and nodded and waved him through back into the school.

Henry hurried along the deserted corridor. The school, normally packed with people and frantic with activity, was empty and quiet and suddenly felt quite spooky. Henry felt ashamed of being a little frightened and reassured himself with the thought that Mr Yale was just within earshot down near the door waiting to let him out. Suddenly Henry saw that Mr Z's door was slightly ajar and he could hear voices in what sounded like a heated discussion. He tiptoed nearer to the door, overcome with curiosity.

'... you've just got to get your act together, Zdradzacski,' a voice was saying. 'You promised me your team would lose against St Mediocre's and you won seven – four. Great! My boy was *gutted*. Well you'll get no fee for this result and if this carries on I'll be taking the car back!'

Henry couldn't believe his ears, Z-man was being paid to fix matches and his new flash car had been a bribe. But who on earth could afford to give away a car like that just to win a football match? He had to know. His heart pounding so hard he was afraid they might hear it, he crept, ever so slowly, to the door. There was a square of reinforced glass in the centre of the door with a little curtain inside. The curtain wasn't quite concealing the window and Henry cautiously peeped through the gap. To his relief nobody in the room was facing the door. Z-man had his back to the door and two other men on either side of him were sitting facing each other. Henry instantly recognised the man who was talking and gave an involuntary gasp. It was Obama Podpilasky, the owner of one of the most famous clubs in the country!

'Look!' Mr Z sounded flustered. More than flustered, thought Henry – he sounded downright scared. 'Look,' he repeated, 'Saturday's result was a one-off. It was utterly bizarre. The two boys I bribed did everything they could to lose, but another wretched little striker did astonishingly well.' Henry at first felt a frisson of pleasure – he had no doubt who the 'wretched little striker' was and was delighted to have thwarted Z-man's plans and caused him so much grief – but this was followed by a pang of apprehension as he thought about the possible implications of this. 'There was nothing I could do. I did keep Sharp – the good striker – on the bench until I thought St Mediocre's were far enough ahead, but then he did brilliantly well and won the match. I wasn't the referee, so I had no control over the game.'

'I'm not paying you to have no control,' Podpilasky hissed. 'This isn't a game – this is deadly serious. Now Alan here,' he nodded to his companion whom Henry didn't recognise, 'tells me that you've got two matches booked in the next fortnight and to fit in with our – ahem – arrangements it's *essential* you win them. And we want exact scores: three–nil next week and five–nil the week after. Two weeks today I'll see you here: same time, same place and if you've won both matches – with the right scores – everybody will be very happy and you'll be considerably richer. If you *haven't*, everybody will be very *unhappy*, but ...' his voice took on a sinister note that made Henry shudder, '... but *you* will be considerably unhappier than anyone else – if you get my meaning.' Henry couldn't see Z-man's face but from his stuttered, mumbling reply he had no doubt that he did indeed get his meaning.

'W ... why the exact scores?' he heard Oskar ask in a trembling voice, something Henry himself was wondering.

'Never you mind,' snarled Podpilasky, but then he softened slightly – he did, after all, want to keep this man on side. He managed a weak smile. 'Just call it the whim of a very rich man.' He took a crocodile-skin case out of his top pocket and started to put on his dark glasses. 'Right! Time to go.' Henry realised in panic that he couldn't possibly risk getting caught – but he daren't run for fear of making a noise. Nearby was the large wicker basket used for lost property. He crept over to it, raised the lid, and climbed in. The lid made a tiny squeak as he lowered it just as the men came out of the room.

'What was that?' asked Lackey. Henry could just see them through the cracks in the basketwork. The three looked up and down the corridor. Henry hardly dared breathe.

'Probably a mouse,' said Z-man, relieved not to be the centre of attention any more. 'The place is running with them. Bits of kids' lunches all over the place!' The three of them went off down the corridor and Henry breathed a sigh of relief. His hands were damp with sweat and his pulse was racing.

After several minutes had passed, Henry eventually plucked up the courage to emerge. He looked cautiously up and down and then dashed into his classroom, grabbed his maths homework, and hurried to the door, watching out all the time for Z-man. The caretaker was leaning against the doorpost reading a racing newspaper and smoking.

'I'm really sorry, Mr Yale,' said Henry, 'I ... I had to go to the toilet.'

'That's OK, son,' said Mr Yale who was fond of Henry. 'Had to hang around because Mr Z's only just left. He had some posh visitors.' He lowered his voice and said, conspiratorially, 'Shifty looking blokes if you ask me – but nobody did ask me, so they'll never know!' He laughed at his witticism and Henry politely laughed as well before thanking him again and scurrying off. He was relieved to see that the black limousine and Z-man's car had both gone and for the first time in the last twenty minutes or so began to relax again. He couldn't wait to tell the others what he had discovered. No wonder Alfie had reassured them all not to worry about receiving help from the elves to win matches. They must have known all along that evil was afoot between Podpilasky and Z-man.

'The lid made a tiny squeak as he lowered it.'

7

A Council of War

The boys sat in Ben's bedroom. Ben and Christopher had listened, spellbound, to Henry's account of his eavesdropping adventure and he had had to repeat every word of the overheard conversation again and again. Downstairs, Jane wondered what was going on. There had been no fighting and she had heard no arguments. Maybe, at last, she thought, they were just learning to get on with their homework without being cajoled, bribed or shouted at. She thought about going up to check but decided to let sleeping dogs lie. It was very peaceful and she sat down to check her emails before putting the fish fingers in the oven.

'Hadn't we better tell Mum and Dad?' asked Henry.

'I'm not sure,' said Ben. 'You know what grown-ups are like. They'll think you misheard something or misunderstood what you heard and they wouldn't want to make a fuss unless they were absolutely sure. After all, it's a pretty serious accusation you're making.'

'What about telling Grandma and Grandpa?' said Christopher.

'Same applies to them as to Mum and Dad,' said Ben, ' – and they'd be even less keen to interfere with stuff going on at school: they'd think we'd have to tell Mum and Dad first. I suppose we could have asked Uncle Michael if he wasn't exploring the Himalayas. No, we'll have to leave the grown-ups out of it and concentrate on getting proof. *Real* evidence, like the police do on TV.'

'Time to wash hands for tea, boys.' Jane's voice came floating up from downstairs.

'OK,' said Henry, 'Let's all think about it but we've got to swear not to tell anyone else till we've decided.' They held hands and took a solemn pledge as Ben had read about the Outlaws doing in the *Just William* book he was reading. Then they went down to get ready for tea.

The next day, Henry and Christopher were in the garden chatting with the elf, while Ben was inside doing homework. The boys had being asking Alfie more about his magic powers and had come on to the subject of invisibility.

'Can you make anything you touch invisible?' asked Christopher.

'You can't see my clothes when I disappear, can you?'

'No – o,' agreed Christopher.

'That's because they're touching me – and if I'm carrying something then that becomes invisible too – if I *want* it to, that is. If for some reason I wanted you to see a stick or a ball floating through the air I could carry it and leave it visible even if I became invisible!'

'Wow, that's really cool,' said Christopher.

'And could be really useful too,' added Henry, thoughtfully.

'How?' asked his brother.

'Well, I've been wondering how we expose Z-man and Podpilasky to the police. Even if we told Mum and Dad and they went to the police I bet nobody would believe them. As Ben says, we need proof and I've just had a brilliant idea – but first I have to do an experiment. Wait here!' He dashed inside. Christopher and the elf looked at each other.

'What's he doing?' asked Christopher. The elf shrugged his little shoulders.

'I really have no idea,' he replied with a grin. 'But it sounds interesting!'

A few minutes later Henry came out carrying his phone.

'Right!' he said as he found the voice recorder on the screen, 'sing something, Christie.' Christopher laughed and then sang Happy Birthday. After a few bars Henry told Christopher he could stop. 'Now watch,' he said to the elf, '– or, rather, listen!' He stopped the recording and then pressed play. Christopher's voice started singing the tune again. The elf looked in amazement from the phone to Christopher.

'But you're not singing,' he said.

'No!' laughed Henry, 'the first time he sang, I recorded the notes on my phone and now it's playing them back.'

'That's like magic,' said the elf.

'Not really – it's just clever. But you can do *real* magic and this is my experiment. It kind of mixes up our magic and your magic. Here's what I want to do.' He told Christopher to start singing again and he started to record again. Then he handed the phone to the elf. 'If you don't mind,' he said, 'I'd like you to become invisible – and make the machine invisible and then, after a little while, become visible again. The machine won't hurt you.' The elf, puzzled, took the phone and suddenly both he and the device disappeared. Christopher stopped singing. 'No! –' said Henry, '– carry on singing. Or say anything. We can just talk if you want.'

'OK,' said Christopher. 'What are you up to?'

'You'll see. Now – we've probably said enough. Come back, Alfie!' he called, and the elf immediately reappeared, still clutching the phone. 'Right,' said Henry. 'The moment of truth.' He took back the phone and fiddled with the screen.

'... no,' came Henry's voice from the phone, '... carry on singing. Or say anything. We can just talk if you want ...' He grinned in pleasure and stopped the recording. The elf and Christopher still looked puzzled.

'Don't you see?' said Henry. 'It works! It's wonderful! The phone still records even when it's invisible!' Light dawned on Christopher.

'So that means ... that means we can record people in secret as long as Alfie's there holding the phone.'

'Exactly,' said Henry, 'and that's how we're going to put Z-man and Podpilasky into prison.'

'Hang on!' said Christopher, flushing with excitement. 'I've got another idea. What if we take some video as well. Will that work?' Henry looked impressed.

'Don't see why not – but let's try?' So once again they involved Alfie in an experiment and, sure enough, an invisible phone held by him, took perfectly good photos and video clips. 'This is fantastic,' said Henry. 'Well done Christie! With the sound and the video, we must be able to get them.'

That evening Henry and Christopher told Ben about their exciting ideas following their experiments with Alfie. Henry was worried that Ben would pooh-pooh their plan but to his surprise and pleasure Ben was very supportive.

'It's a brilliant plan,' he said. 'But let me just think about it for a minute.' The others waited patiently, an unusual phenomenon – it was curious how a big and real event such as this had brought them together and changed their behaviour. 'What I think,' Ben said eventually, speaking slowly and carefully, 'is that we should record and video that meeting in two weeks' time. But ...' he continued before the others could respond, '... but we want to be sure there is something *incriminating* for them to say. This is my plan.' He turned to Henry. 'Podpilasky wants two wins in a row – that's what you said isn't it?' Henry nodded. 'OK, well Henry and Alfie and his sibs should try and win next week.'

'Shouldn't be a problem,' said Henry, ' – we're playing Duffer's Prep who are rubbish.'

'Good,' said Ben, 'because we don't want any upset next week. We can't have Podpilasky getting angry and arranging an emergency meeting that we don't know about.'

'Good thinking,' agreed Henry, and Christopher nodded.

'And,' continued Ben, 'make sure the score is right – what was it you said he wants for the first match, Henry, three-nil to us?' Henry nodded. 'And will you be able to fix that score?'

'Yeah, shouldn't be a problem 'cos Wayne and Darren will be trying for that too – we're all on the same side in this match.' He paused, then added. 'And that's something I meant to ask you : why do you think he wants exact scores?'

'Dunno,' said Ben. 'Must be something to do with their scam. Anyway, to get back to your matches, we *do* want him to get mad with Z-man at the meeting they've arranged for the Monday after the second match. So that he says some things that give us evidence. So ...' he paused and looked cautiously at Henry, '... so you'll have to *lose* the match the following Saturday – the one two days before the meeting.' Henry looked horrified.

'But we can't lose that,' he said. 'We just can't. We're playing St Jude's and they're even more rubbish than Duffer's!'

'Hang on! Hang on!' said Ben, 'Let me finish. There are three things to think about. First, as I've already said, we've got to have Podpilasky mad and this is how to do it. Secondly, you don't have to play badly – you can score, say, one or two goals but Alfie can make it so that Wayne and Darren do very badly and your keeper does badly. In that way it looks as if Luigi's lost the match *despite* your good play, not because you played badly. Thirdly, you don't need to worry about St Luigi's place in the league – it's still early in the competition and St Jude's are so rubbish that they probably won't win any more matches. With Alfie's help St Luigi's can easily catch up with any other good teams as the season goes on.'

Henry stared at him, frustrated, but then he gave a resigned smile.

'You're right. Everything you say is true. That is what we'll do – but it's going to be really annoying having to lose to those St Jude's dumbos.'

'Now let's think about what we want on the video,' said Ben. 'We obviously need the three of them talking but it would be good to show their car and chauffeur in the school grounds.'

'Yes,' said Henry. 'That car's got personalised number plates – PODA1 – which every football fan in the country knows about.'

'But we could've just got a picture of the car and put it into the video,' said Christopher. 'Let's get a picture of Podpilasky actually getting in or out of the car at the school.'

'– and without his dark glasses, if possible,' added Henry.

'I'm sure that can be arranged with Alfie,' said Ben. 'Listen, here's an idea.' And they talked and planned until Jane called them down to tea.

At the very same time that the Sharp brothers were planning their tactics, Oskar was sitting late in the PE office going over in his mind the disastrous meeting that had taken place in that very spot the previous evening. He couldn't fail again: it wasn't just the loss of the money and the car – he knew that Podpilasky was a ruthless and powerful man who wouldn't hesitate to send Ron and his cronies round if he felt he had been let down. His mind turned to Henry. If it hadn't been for him they would have lost last week's match and everything would have been fine. The trouble was that Henry was on such good form he couldn't possibly find any excuse to exclude him from the team. The rest of the sports staff, the other boys in the team and the parents would simply find it incredible. As he mulled over the problem he realised that in fact Henry was actually valuable – if not now indispensable – when they were playing matches that Podpilasky *wanted* him to win. Henry, naturally, was going to try and win in every match they played. No, the big problem was going to come when Podpilasky instructed him to *lose* a match. When that happened he'd have to try and keep Henry on the bench for most of the match while Wayne and Darren deliberately played to lose. Though that hadn't been very successful in the last match. That only meant – and he didn't really like to think about this – that he'd have to arrange for Ron to disable Henry in some way. Fortunately the next two matches were both ones that Podpilasky wanted him to win so he could relax for a fortnight and cross that unpleasant bridge when he came to it.

To Oskar's great relief the match against Duffer's Preparatory School the following Saturday went well, St Luigi winning three–nil. Sure enough, late on Monday evening his doorbell rang. On the doorstep was a man carrying a brown paper packet.

'You Zedsky?' he asked.

'Yes, I'm Zdradzacski if that's who you mean.' The man nodded, checked a photo on his phone and looked at Oskar. Satisfied, he handed over the package and without further conversation returned to his car and drove off. As he took the packet indoors Oskar realised that this must be his first payment for a successful result.

The packet was full of crisp new £20 notes and as Oskar feverishly counted the money he became more determined than ever that this arrangement should continue. Next Saturday should be OK because Podpilasky wanted another win and Oskar knew that St Jude's was rubbish. Another fat brown packet should soon be on its way. He did have to ensure that the score was exactly five–nil but the other team was so bad he was sure that Wayne and Darren could make this happen. It had, after all, worked perfectly in the recent match. Once they reached five goals he would substitute Henry so he didn't score any more.

On Thursday, after football practice, the Gormless boys each found a brown envelope tucked into their sports bags and they too looked forward to further easy money in the week to come. That same day an invisible Alfie had accompanied Christopher to school and been shown where Oskar's office was.

On Saturday the league match against St Jude's was again a home fixture for St Luigi's, making an easy win even more likely. Ben's own fixture had been cancelled so he was able to watch the match with the rest of the family.

Henry and Wayne were the forwards with Darren and Adam in midfield, Dominic and Joshua as backs, and Max as usual in goal. Wayne was full of confidence and was even cordial to Henry for a change, high-fiving him as they stood waiting to start. This should be a piece of cake, he thought, and another envelope would be in his sports bag next week.

Henry was nervous about how easy it would be to actually lose the game – the first time he had ever been in such a situation – but in the event he need not have worried. Alfie had brought thirteen invisible companions with him, one to mark every player on the field and they did a fantastic job. Henry had decided the best stratagem was to appear to be a generous player, so during the match he repeatedly passed the ball to Wayne or back to Darren whenever there seemed a good opportunity for Luigi's to score. But Wayne and Darren seemed to have mystifyingly bad luck that day. Every goal shot seemed to curve into a goal post, over the top, or into the St Jude's' goalkeeper's waiting arms.

And the St Jude's strikers were on top form. The ball seemed to cling to their boots as if by magic, their shots at goal curved brilliantly into the net – even those that at first looked certain to miss, and on two occasions when a shot seemed an easy catch for Max the ball seemed to hit lumps of mud or turf and bounce away from him into the back of the net. Five minutes before the final whistle a striker dribbled with mysterious ease past Wayne, Adam and Joshua and scored with a shot that seemed simply to curve around Max into the net. The score was now five–nil to St Jude's.

The visiting team's parents and supporters went wild with delight and St Luigi's were dumbfounded at being thrashed by one of the worst teams in the league. Mr Z, who wasn't refereeing the match, was standing near the St Jude's goal pale with anger and fear. To add to his discomfiture he overheard one of the St Luigi parents criticising Wayne and Darren:

'That Sharp boy has set them up for easy goals time and again and they've just thrown their opportunities away. Sharp could have scored a dozen goals if he hadn't been too generous to his team mates.'

Now, as the match drew to a close, the elves changed their tactics at a pre-arranged signal from Ben. In the final moments of the game Henry swept through St Jude's' defences and scored two brilliant goals. Beside him on the touchline Oskar heard the same parent talking to his wife.

'There, told you so, he should have kept the ball and done that all through the match instead of wasting those fantastic passes on the Gormless boys.'

The final whistle blew just as Henry slammed in a third goal. This was initially disallowed by the line judge because Henry had been marginally offside, but the referee reminded the linesman that there was no offside rule in the seven-a-side matches so the final score was five–three to St Jude's.

Henry turned and looked at Ben and Christopher on the touch line with their parents. Jane and Marcus were downcast but couldn't understand why the boys didn't seem more disappointed. Henry gave his brothers a quick grin and then turned back to console his team mates as Oskar stumbled from the field in horrified disbelief.

'You don't seem very upset, love,' said Jane to Christopher.

'Well Henry played such a brilliant game that the final result didn't really matter,' he replied. 'Wayne and Darren lost the game for us – and the St Jude's goalie was fantastic so they deserved to win.'

'Yeah, that's what I think,' added Ben.

'That's a very mature analysis,' said Marcus. 'And I'm really pleased you're such good sports you're able to see it that way. I'm sure St. Luigi's will make up for it as the season goes on.'

'The final whistle blew just as Henry slammed in a third goal.'

8

Collecting Damning Evidence

The boys spent the rest of the weekend in a state of nervous excitement. Ben had spent his birthday money on buying the smallest possible phone to make it easier for Alfie to manipulate and Alfie had practised with it at the end of the garden under the boys' supervision.

Much as they wanted to see what went on after school on Monday they didn't dare hang around in case Z-man saw them and became suspicious. When Mr Z went back to his office at the end of the after-school club Henry walked out of school and then waited on a street corner nearby until he saw the black limousine purr down the road and turn into the school. Then he ran home and joined the others. From now on it was up to Alfie and his team.

Alfie, invisible of course, filmed the limousine coming up the school drive. He stood in a spot Henry had chosen with him during the previous week which gave a good view of both the car's unique number plate and the noticeboard with the school's name. The chauffeur opened the car doors and as Podpilasky got out Ariel, one of Alfie's invisible team and his favourite elfsib, flew up and spattered his dark glasses with mud.

Cursing, and looking round in bewilderment to see where the mud had come from, Podpilasky took off his glasses and wiped them clean with a silk handkerchief. Alfie had moved in for a close-up and got a great shot of Podpilasky's face with the school's name on a wall in the background. Podpilasky and Lackey then marched into the school and went straight to Oskar's office. By the time they were settled in their seats the elves were already recording every sight and sound. Half-an-hour later the two visitors left the ashen-faced teacher slumped in his chair and got back into their car. They had no idea that sitting comfortably on the leather seat opposite them Alfie and Ariel started once again to record everything they did and said.

The following day, as luck would have it, was an inset day at St Luigi's. When Jane dropped them off at their grandparents' house on her way to work the boys couldn't wait to watch and hear the recordings Alfie had made. They had arranged for the elf to meet them in the garden that morning. Grandpa had gone up to London for the day for a meeting and Grandma was only too happy for the boys to play outside by themselves. To her surprise, after a very short game of football, they came in and announced they were going to watch a DVD because it was starting to rain.

Grandma looked out. It was grey but didn't actually seem to be raining, and the boys usually stayed outside until they got absolutely soaked. But she was just as happy for them to be indoors, so the boys settled themselves in front of the television and Ben connected up his smartphone. Alfie and Ariel, invisible in case Grandma came in, sat on a pouf in front of the television.

The video started with the shots of the car and the boys applauded with delight as Podpilasky had to take his glasses off. Then the scene changed to Oskar's office.

Podpilasky was white with anger.

'Just what the hell do you think you're playing at?' he shouted at Oskar.

'I'm paying you a fortune to fix matches and even with you bribing two of your best strikers you can't even win a match against a team you told me was rubbish.' The watching boys couldn't believe their luck. In just one sentence, Podpilasky seemed already to have said enough to incriminate both himself and Z-man. But that was just the start.

'It's absolutely pathetic,' Podpilasky continued – he was so angry the boys could actually see flecks of spit coming out of his mouth as he shouted at Oskar, 'Alan here was watching the match and he says that the two strikers you were bribing to win the match were actually the players who *lost* it and –' his lip curled sarcastically, '– the one striker you *weren't* bribing, the little red-headed genius, was the one who could actually have won the match if he hadn't been let down by the other two! Unbelievable!

Absolutely, flipping, unbelievable!' He paused for breath and leaned forward, his nose just inches away from Oskar's bloodless face. 'Now listen,' he hissed. 'This is your last chance. If any match – *any* match doesn't end up the way Alan tells you it should, you're finished. And –' he added ominously, his voice now low and threatening, '– I don't just mean the arrangements are finished. I mean *you* are finished. Get it?'

At this point Alfie had panned in to Oskar's face and it was clear to the boys that he certainly got it. His eyes were staring out of his pallid face, there were great beads of sweat on his forehead, and his lips were trembling. He tried to speak, but only a croak came out, so he just nodded.

'Now for the wins, I want that red-headed kid in the team,' Podpilasky went on, 'but the next time Lackey wants you to *lose* a match, he's not to play, understand?' Oskar nodded again. 'Get Ron Pollard to fix him – for good if necessary. I want no more mistakes. My son is very upset by what has happened so far.'

The office video ended shortly after and the boys looked at each other as Ben paused the recording.

'What's that about fixing Henry?' said Christopher with a very worried expression. 'Will they hurt him?'

'No,' said Alfie who had been silent so far. 'No, we won't let that happen.'

'Thank you,' said Henry who was looking distinctly apprehensive.

'Yes, thanks,' said Ben. 'And to make quite sure, I think it's time to get our cousins involved.' His brothers looked mystified. What did the cousins have to do with it? 'I'm going to think about it and I'll explain everything to you later,' said Ben. It hadn't escaped his notice that Alfie remained silent. How much did the elf know about Lucy and Grace he wondered – he was, after all, a magical being? 'In the meantime.' he continued, 'we need to see the car video!' As he went to reset the smartphone Henry said.

'What's this about Podpilasky's son? What's he got to do with the match fixing?'

'I think he goes to Ingots School,' said Christopher. 'I read about it in Football News. His dad gave the school enough money to build a new sports hall.'

'That could be it,' said Ben. 'Maybe he's desperate for his school to win the league after his dad's put all that money into the school.' They all agreed that this was the most likely explanation as Ben put on the next video. As it started Alfie spoke again, proud to use one of his colloquial phrases.

'If you thought the office video was damning, you haven't seen anything yet!' Intrigued, the boys stared intently as the interior of Podpilasky's car came on the screen.

The door opened and Grandma looked in.

'It's awfully quiet in here. It must be a good film!' She glanced at the screen as Ben hurriedly paused the video.

'Er, yes,' he said. 'These guys are baddies,' he pointed to Podpilasky and Lackey, confident that the chances of Grandma recognising the world-famous Podpilasky were zero, 'and we're just at an exciting bit.' Grandma laughed.

'OK, I know when I'm not wanted. Let me know when you'd like a biscuit.' To her astonishment, for the first time ever, none of them said he'd like one right now. It *must* be a good film she thought, as she went back out and quietly closed the door.

'Right,' said Ben. 'Let's go.' The video restarted, to show Podpilasky cursing and brushing his trouser leg with a silk handkerchief. Alfie chuckled.

'Ariel decided to throw some mud onto his trousers as he got in the car,' he explained. 'And he's put a spell on it,' he added, as Podpilasky rubbed even more vigorously and furiously at his expensive suit, 'so it won't come off in a hurry.' The boys all clapped and laughed, but soon stopped as Podpilasky started to speak.

'That bloody oaf Zdradzacski has no idea how much this has cost us.' As he spoke he pressed a button and a reinforced glass screen slid across the car so that the chauffeur could not hear their conversation. He turned to Lackey. 'Remind me just how much it was.' His companion nodded as he did some rapid calculations on his phone.

'Well,' he said after a few moments, 'we've now played three league games and Zdradzacski got it wrong in two of them. In those games I estimate that the two dozen gambling syndicates we've set up to run bets on schools matches each lost an average of approximately ten thousand pounds. Some outlets lost less but others much more. Our betting shop in Dubai, for instance, lost just under fifty grand and the Seoul shop thirty grand. Total losses for the company are over three hundred grand.'

'That's serious money,' said Podpilasky thoughtfully. As he spoke, he seemed to the fascinated watching boys to be a little more relaxed than he had been back in the office when he was castigating Z-man. Or was it their imagination? Then, as if he were in the room with them reading their thoughts, Lackey spoke again, somewhat tentatively.

'If ... if you don't mind me saying so, you don't seem quite as annoyed as you should be at these figures.' To the boys' surprise and, from his expression, obviously to Lackey's surprise as well, Podpilasky laughed and slapped his knee.

'No, I suppose I don't. That's because I'm not!' Lackey looked puzzled and Podpilasky went on to explain. 'First of all, the figures show that there is a fantastic interest in betting on school football. This is the first time it's been tried and obviously there are thousands of gamblers out there who are interested. And,' he continued, 'on reflection it may not be a bad thing that the punters have won a lot of money in these early matches, even though it's cost us. They will think that betting on school football is an easy way to make money so they'll be more inclined to place heavier bets and tell all their mates. Then, whenever St Luigi's play, we'll fix the match – either to win or lose, or for the game to end in a specific score. All our betting shops will fix the odds accordingly and we'll make a fortune.'

'Fantastic,' said Lackey. 'So our losses last month have been a kind of investment?'

'Exactly,' replied Podpilasky with a self-satisfied smile. 'That idiot Zdradzacski has actually done us a favour. All the punters are now going to want to make some easy money on school football – and they're soon going to get a nasty shock.'

As their conversation drifted on to other scams and deals the recording came to an end. Ben turned to the pouf where he knew the invisible elves were sitting.

'Well thanks, Alfie and Ariel, that was brilliant.' The others chorused their agreement. 'We'll keep all this evidence in a safe place until we decide how to use it,' Ben continued. 'I'm a bit worried about keeping it on my phone in case I lose it and somebody else finds it. Where's the best place to hide a copy of it?'

'Simple,' said Alfie, 'put it where you want and I'll make it invisible – and protected by a magic barrier. Only the Littlefolk can see it and they won't know what it is and won't be interested in it. Anyway, none of them would come into your house in normal circumstances.'

'Great,' said Ben. 'That solves that problem.'

'I've got some questions too,' said Christopher. 'What are punters?'

'They are gamblers – people who place bets on events like horse races and football matches,' said Ben.

'And I don't understand all this stuff about odds and betting.'

'You don't really need to understand all of it,' said Ben, kindly. 'Podpilasky and Lackey and Z-man are all crooks. Podpilasky and Lackey run betting shops where people – the punters – can bet on the results of football matches. If Podpilasky and Lackey know beforehand what the exact result of a match is going to be then they can con the punters and make millions of pounds over a season. Does that help?'

'Yep,' said Christopher. 'What a scam!' He thought for a moment then said. 'So if Z-man wants a particular result and Henry manages to get a different result, even just a different score, then the crooks lose money instead of winning it?'

'Exactly,' said Ben. 'That's why we're so lucky to have Alfie helping us – and we're all saving thousands of people from being diddled.'

'And now *I've* got a question,' said Henry. 'What were you saying about the cousins, Ben, and how can they possibly help?

Just then the door opened and Grandma appeared. She saw the blank TV screen.

'Good, your film's over. Time to wash your hands for lunch. It's almost ready – Oh, and Grandpa rang to say his meeting finished early and he's on his way back, so we're all going out somewhere this afternoon.' She went back to the kitchen. Ben looked relieved at the interruption and the fact their meeting wouldn't continue that day.

'I'll tell you about the cousins tomorrow,' he said. 'It's a long story but nothing to worry about. Let's go and get ready for lunch.'

That night Ben lay awake and pondered over what to do next. He was worried about what Podpilasky had said about Henry in the videos. There seemed to be no doubt that if it became necessary for the sake of their scheme they would have no hesitation in injuring or even killing Henry. Alfie had reassured them that Henry would be safe and Ben knew that he had considerable powers. On the other hand, Alfie had also told the boys that the elves were forbidden by the ancient Faerie Code from physically harming the Greatfolk in any way and Ben had correctly guessed that the 'Ron' referred to by Podpilasky was an extremely unpleasant and ruthless character. He had a strong instinct that he should now involve his cousins to be absolutely certain of ensuring his brother's safety. Ben had only recently learnt something amazing about his cousin, Lucy.*

A few weeks earlier, during the summer holidays, Ben and his cousin Sarah had gone to East Africa. While on safari they had been taken hostage by poachers but they had been rescued by Lucy and it was then that Ben had learnt of her extraordinary power. He had known for some time previously that there was something unusual about Lucy but didn't know exactly what it was, just that she got on very well with animals – any animals. What he had not known until then, for it had been a family secret, was that Lucy could actually *speak* to animals and animals would do her bidding. She had used this power to rescue Sarah and Ben and, in a further extraordinary twist to the tale, had found her twin sister, Grace, long ago believed to have been killed, who shared the same ability as Lucy to speak to animals.

Please see Prologue for full details.

During their African adventure and rescue Ben and Sarah had obviously learnt the truth about both Lucy and Grace but had agreed with the rest of the family that Henry and Christopher would not be told the secret until they were older. This was to protect both them and the girls.

Now, as Ben tossed and turned, he was in a quandary. He desperately needed advice and help, and he had seen with his own eyes the effects of the power that Lucy and Grace possessed. If they knew about Henry there could be no possibility of his being harmed by anyone because they could call upon any animals to protect him. On the other hand, could he tell his cousins about the elf secret he now shared with Henry and Christopher and could he share with his brothers all that he knew about his cousins? Eventually he fell into a fitful sleep.

9

Conversations with Cousins

As is so often the case, things seemed clearer to Ben in the morning. He woke early, despite his bad night, and immediately decided on his plan of action. His first duty had to be to protect his brother. After school when all three brothers were in the garden he spoke to the others.

'Look, I know we agreed that Alfie and the football scam would be our secret, and that we wouldn't tell the grown-ups. But I'm the eldest and I'd like to talk to somebody else about what's going on. If I swear them to secrecy do you mind if I talk to the girls about this?' Henry and Christopher looked at each other. Henry shrugged his shoulders.

'To be honest, I'd be quite glad if they knew. I'm feeling a bit … scared by the whole thing.'

'Me too,' said Christopher. 'Go for it!' When they went inside Ben asked Jane if he could go to tea with Sarah the next day. She didn't mind as long as it was OK with Joanna, so Ben rang Sarah and fixed it up. Clare was away at university but he checked that Lucy and Grace would be there as well. The next day he spoke to the three of them in their garden after tea.

'Look, I've got something incredible to tell you, guys.' He paused. 'It's so complicated I don't know where to begin.'

'How about the beginning?' said Lucy, gently. 'We've got all evening.' Ben laughed.

'OK, here goes. You know Christie banged his head and went to hospital?' They all nodded. Then Lucy interrupted:

'Just a minute. I heard Mum talking to Auntie Jane about this. Didn't they find out that Christie had a large pineal gland?'

'Dunno,' said Ben. 'But they said he was OK. What's with this gland?'

'Well only that Clare told me that *I* had a large pineal gland and I was just wondering ...' Her voice tailed off. 'Sorry, I interrupted your story. Go on.'

'Well, the day Christie got back from hospital, he was in the garden and then something amazing happened. Lucy and Grace exchanged glances.

'Don't tell me,' said Lucy, 'an animal started to talk to him.' Ben couldn't help grinning even though it was such a serious matter.

'No – o,' he said. He paused for dramatic effect. It certainly worked. The three girls were consumed with curiosity. 'No, an *elf* started to talk to him. An elf dressed in a football club strip!'

'An elf!' exclaimed Grace. She looked at Lucy. 'I didn't think they existed! Have you ever seen an elf?' Lucy shook her head and turned to Ben with a smile.

'Are you sure he isn't having you on? He loves a joke.'

'Quite sure,' said Ben. 'I've seen the elf myself – and so's Henry.' There was a stunned silence, broken eventually by Lucy.

'Then ...' she began slowly, '... then it's difficult to believe that Christie doesn't have something similar to me and Grace – especially with this thing about his head injury and the pineal gland.'

'Yes,' agreed Sarah, 'if he had just told us this and we didn't know about you two,' she nodded at Lucy and Grace, 'we would think he was crazy or making it up. But as we do know about you guys and your pineal gland, Lucy – he must just have a similar, but different power.'

'I'm sure you're both right,' said Grace. 'Otherwise it's just too much of a coincidence.' She paused. 'I just wonder if Lucy and I could talk to the elves too – but I've never felt the slightest message from them.' She looked enquiringly at her twin, who shook her head.

'I'd love to talk about this with Grandpa,' said Lucy. 'I think that Christie's pineal must be receiving messages on a different part of the electromagnetic spectrum than we use.' She suddenly turned to Ben. 'Can the elves talk to the animals?'

'I dunno,' said Ben. 'Christie might know – he's spent a lot of time talking to them. Anyway, I know you are interested in science and all that but we're getting off the point. The point is that the elves *can* speak to Christie and we've discovered something really dodgy that has put Henry in danger.' He then told them the whole story about Mr Z (whom Sarah already knew – she had been in Ben's year at St Luigi's) and Podpilasky, Lackey and Ron Pollard. When he had finished there was a shocked silence for a few seconds. Then Lucy spoke.

'I know exactly what to do,' she said – she paused and looked at Grace, who nodded: the twins were attuned with each other's thoughts, '– but I'd like to talk to Clare – is that OK?' Ben nodded.

'Before you say what your plan is,' said Grace to Lucy, 'there is a problem. I don't think we can stop Henry and Christopher from knowing about you and me. Henry needs to know so he feels safe, and Christopher needs to know because we can't talk to the elves without him.' Lucy nodded.

'I think you're right, but it *is* a problem. Mum and Dad and Grandpa and Grandma didn't want them to know until they were older – just as we didn't tell Sarah and Ben at first.'

'But you *did* tell us,' Sarah interrupted, 'because you *had* to when we got kidnapped in Africa – otherwise you'd probably have left it till we were thirteen or fourteen. And now you *have* to tell Henry and Christopher because of what's happened to *them*.'

'You're right,' said Lucy and Grace nodded in agreement. 'We've no choice but to tell them now. OK, now that's settled, my plan is to set up a 24-hour foolproof protection system for Henry with the animals. I'll need to know a few more details about Podpilasky and Ron but I can ask you later – by the way, did you say Ron *Pollard*?' Ben nodded.

'Why – do you know him?' he asked.

'I knew *someone* called Pollard. Someone rather nasty – but I'm sure it's just a coincidence. Anyway, to get back to the point, we don't want to upset the elves because they have been so kind to you: I'll must reassure them we're not trying to push in or take over. I have to talk to this Alfie, so I'll need Christie to act as an interpreter.' Already Ben felt an immense sense of relief washing over him. Until this moment he hadn't realised the strain that being the eldest of the boys had placed upon him. The involvement of his cousins and, above all, Lucy's supreme confidence, made him feel that a great weight had been lifted from his shoulders. He thanked his cousins and went off home, planning what he should tell his brothers.

The girls had been fascinated by Ben's story and as soon as he had left Lucy turned to the cat Tibbles, who had been sitting under Sarah's garden chair during Ben's visit. From her experience in Africa Sarah immediately recognised the faraway look on her sister's face that meant she was talking to an animal. Lucy was consumed with curiosity to know if the animals knew about the elves.

'What is your wish, Promised One?' asked the cat, immediately sensing the fact that Lucy was communicating with her.

'We have spoken to Bennikin as you saw,' said Lucy, *'and he tells us that Christiekin has some power akin to my own.'* The cat, who knew all the boys, pricked up her ears and became very interested.

'Can he speak to me as thou canst?' she asked.

'No,' started Lucy but, suddenly realising she didn't actually know the answer to that question, added, *'at least I think not. But he can speak to some other beings who live in the woods and have great power. Dost thou know of such creatures?'*

'We do think there are others who live in the woods,' replied Tibbles. *'None of my kin has ever seen such creatures but we often smell them nearby when the brilliant one sleeps and we have no doubt that they are there. We call them the Hiddenkin. And ...'* she hesitated.

'And ...?' encouraged Lucy.

'... and it is said that there is a legend among the nightbanes that in ancient times – before the Tailless Ones ruled the earth – these creatures came out from their shadow during sunsleep and could be seen dancing in the light of the Great Silver One. 'Tis said that they looked like tailless ones yet were only the size of a hedgiquill or a coneyhop.' Tibbles saw Lucy about to ask more questions and forestalled her. *'But these are matters beyond the ken of a furriclaws, O Promised One. To know more thou shouldst once again speak to others.'*

Sarah was beside herself with impatience, having watched Lucy and Grace gazing at Tibbles and knowing they were conversing.

'Come on you two! That's long enough! Don't be mean! What did she say? Has she seen an elf? Can she talk to them?'

Lucy and Grace laughed.

'Sorry, we should have translated as we went along,' said Lucy. 'Anyway, it's really exciting. The animals know of the elves but only because they can smell them – they can't

'...and it is said that...these creatures came out from their shadows during sunsleep and could be seen dancing in the light of the Great Silver One...'

see them. At least not nowadays. There's a legend that they used to be visible to the animals long, long ago but Tibbles says I need to speak to other animals to find out more.'

'What animals?' asked Sarah.

'Well,' said Lucy, 'when I first discovered I could speak to animals I wanted to find out why they called me 'The Promised One' and the only animals that could really help me were the dolphins and the monkeys. Then, when I went to Africa there were these chimpanzees which were incredibly intelligent – they were really easy to talk to. They were called…'

'Bonobos,' interrupted Sarah, 'Just in case you don't remember I was there, silly, and saw you and Grace talking to them!' Grace looked a little sad as she remembered her childhood and the wonderful experiences she had had with these gentle and intelligent animals in the Congo.

'Anyway,' said Lucy. 'Finding out what the animals really know about the elves is an interesting project for the future. The urgent thing now is to protect Henry and for that I need to talk to Christopher and his elf friends.'

'What did the girls say?' asked Henry when the boys were able to sit and talk together.

'Well,' said Ben, 'we've all agreed that we should keep the grown-ups out of this for the moment. Lucy's agreed to meet with Alfie and discuss with him his plans for protecting Henry to see if she thinks they're OK.' He stopped to gather his thoughts. 'And now there's something really special I've got to tell you. Do you remember when Sarah and I got rescued last year in Africa?'

'Of course,' said Henry, and Christopher nodded in agreement.

'Well what you *didn't* know was that it was mainly because of Lucy. You know how good she is with animals?' They both nodded vigorously. They had seen countless examples of animals being extraordinarily friendly with Lucy – savage-looking dogs, unfriendly-looking cats, even wild animals like the deer and rabbits in Richmond Park and birds in the garden. 'Well,' continued Ben, 'she can really get animals to do anything she wants but Mum and Dad and Joanna and Richard don't talk about it and don't want us to talk about it.'

'Are you saying,' Henry said, 'she can *talk* to animals?'

'Well ... yes,' said Ben. 'And more than that, they have a kind of ancient legend about her. They've been expecting her to appear for ages and ages and think she's going to restore a kind of better relationship between humans and animals. They regard her so highly that they'll do anything she asks them to do – *anything*!' Henry and Christopher were speechless for a long moment as they tried to absorb the incredible facts they had just heard. But Ben hadn't finished. 'And Grace can talk to animals as well – because they're identical twins – and the forest animals in Africa treated her as being special, just like Lucy.'

'Wow, that's so cool!' said Christopher eventually.

'It's ... unbelievable,' said Henry. 'Are you kidding us?'

'No,' said Ben, 'and I'm only telling you this now because we need her help to protect you, Henry. So it's a massive, massive, *unbreakable* family secret. Yeah?'

'Yeah,' they both said, slightly awed by how serious Ben sounded.

'Thanks for telling us,' said Henry. 'I know Alfie's clever and can do magic stuff but I still feel happier knowing that Lucy and Grace are going to help him.'

'Good, and so do I,' said Ben. 'That's settled then. We'll get the cousins to come round so Lucy can make some plans with Alfie, and you ...' he turned to Christopher, '... are vital in this because you're the only one who can speak to him.'

And so, two days later Jane, at the boys' request, invited the girls round and immediately after tea all six children disappeared outside. She wondered what they were doing: Sarah and the boys usually played football but they all seemed to be sitting chatting on the climbing frame at the end of the garden.

'Are you there Alfie?' called Christopher. 'It's OK to come out.'

'I'm here already,' said a little voice, and to the girls' utter astonishment the elf materialised. He was sitting on a rung of the climbing frame between Lucy and Sarah and the boys were amused to see that as a courteous gesture to the visiting cousins he was dressed in the strip of a famous northern club – Sarah's favourite team. Christopher recalled that he had mentioned this to Alfie during one of their football discussions and was impressed that elf had remembered.

'Alfie, these are my cousins, Lucy, Grace and Sarah,' said Christopher, pointing to each of them in turn. The girls all smiled and waved politely in greeting, and the elf stood up on the rail, swept his hat off and bowed to each in turn as he said hello. Henry explained that they could speak to Alfie but only hear *him* speak if Christopher was present. Lucy was immediately curious to know if she could communicate with the elf on her own. She asked him to carry on speaking and then asked Christopher to move away. After he had gone about ten yards the elf's voice suddenly cut out. Lucy felt a pang of disappointment. She had hoped against hope she would be able to converse directly with the elf – not only to help Henry, but also because the notion of being able to talk to a creature almost certainly more intelligent and knowledgeable than any animal was mind-blowing. She glanced surreptitiously at Grace who shook her head, almost imperceptibly. They both knew that neither of them could hear the elf. Lucy's favourite subjects were maths and physics and she knew immediately that the elf must be communicating with Christopher on a waveband in the electromagnetic spectrum that she was unable to access. But then she had another idea: she thought she would try and communicate with him as she did with the animals. She gazed at the elf who was now sitting down again. From her expression Ben and Sarah both knew instantly that she was trying to talk to him.

'Knowest thou the common tongue?' she asked. There was a breathless pause that reminded Lucy of the first time she had spoken to a dinosaur in an Amazon crater. Then both she and Grace became aware of a sound signal – a wash of static crackle almost exactly like the sound emitted by an untuned radio. Soon, magically, the static cleared and a tiny tinkling voice spoke, very slowly and hesitantly.

'I ... do ... understand ... thee ... but ... to ... speak ... to ... thee ... is ... very ... hard.' A long pause, then: 'Though ... we ... *can* ... speak ... the ... common ... tongue ... we ... converse ... not ... with ... the ... Furrykin ... and ... the ... Feathered folk.' Another pause, then he added: 'It ... is ... easier ... to ... speak ... to ... Christopher ... in ... the... elven ... tongue ... *much* ... easier!'

The others stood patiently waiting and Lucy gave them a thumbs up sign as she turned to explain:

'He understands me but he hardly ever speaks in the universal ancient language and would much rather talk through Christie.' She was very relieved – at least in an emergency she and Grace could talk to the elf, albeit very slowly, without Christopher being present. Now she spoke aloud for she knew the elf readily understood normal human language and waved to Christopher to return so that the elf could also answer easily.

'I am the Promised One,' she said to the elf, 'and my sister –' she pointed to Grace, '– assists me in my task.' Christopher was now back in range and she could hear the elf speaking fluently again.

'All the Littlefolk know of thee from ancient lore and we know of thy great powers with the Furrykin and other creatures. I am honoured to meet you.'

'Thank you,' said Lucy. 'Now Henry is in danger and I know you can protect him – but if it will help you in this task I can instruct any creatures to do whatever you require.' The elf didn't seem the slightest put out by her offer of help.

'Your offer of help is of great value to me and my elfsibs and I am sure we will use it to protect your cousin.'

'This so cool,' said Sarah.

'Yeah,' agreed Ben. 'We've sorted out so much in just a few minutes.'

And on that satisfactory note they all thanked the elf, who promptly disappeared. The boys started a game of football and the girls went home – followed, unknown to them, by an invisible elf who wanted to see where they lived in case he needed urgent help from the animals.

A few days later the six cousins were having another council of war.

'When should we show our video stuff to the grown-ups?' asked Ben. 'We've already got enough evidence to get them into trouble haven't we?'

'Yes,' said Lucy. 'I'm sure that bribing a teacher and threatening to hurt people must be offences but the police might be able to charge them with much more if we delay things a bit. If they are diddling gamblers in their betting shops then every time they fix a match they must be getting deeper into trouble.'

'Yes, as long as that doesn't put Henry at risk,' said Sarah.

'I think Henry's OK as long as they want St Luigi's to win – they know he's their best player,' said Lucy, 'they'll only try to stop him playing if they want St Luigi's to lose – and then Alfie and the animals will protect him.'

'How will we know when they're planning to fix the matches,' said Henry. 'They're not going to tell me.'

'Well we have no idea of when or how Lackey will contact Z-man,' said Lucy. 'But we can probably – with Alfie's help – check on when Z-man tells the – what are they called?'

'Gormless,' said Henry.

'Yes, the Gormless boys, and Alfie can record those conversations. Let's go out and see if he'll have time to do all this.' They went out into the garden and Christopher called the elf who appeared within a few seconds. After they had told him their plans Christopher asked him if he would have enough time to sit in Z-man's office all week.

'Time!' laughed the elf. Time is nothing to us. We have no work to do and we live for hundreds and hundreds of your years. Time is whatever we choose it to be whether it's a second or a day or a year. And, don't forget, we can take it in turns – several times day or even an hour if we want.'

'But how will you tell your elfsibs when you want a break? Can you speak to each other from afar as we do with our machines?'

'No,' laughed the elf. 'We can fly!'

'Of course,' said Christopher, 'I'd quite forgotten that.' He paused. 'How *fast* can you fly?'

'We fly like the twinkling of an eye,' the elf replied. Christopher wasn't sure just how fast this was, but it seemed rude to press the point and 'the twinkling of an eye' didn't sound like anything very slow. 'There is one other thing,' the elf continued. 'I want to know whenever Lackey contacts this Ron Pollard because he is the man who they are going to use to try and 'fix' people. As long as we know what Lackey tells Pollard we can be sure of using Lucy's animals to keep Henry safe from harm.'

'Good thinking,' said Lucy, 'but how can you do that as well as everything else – and how will you know where to go?'

'There are many, many elfsibs and we can easily keep watch on Lackey,' replied the elf. 'As for where to go – don't forget that I went with Podpilasky and Lackey in their car when they returned to their club from meeting Z-man at St Luigi's. I can tell the elfsibs exactly where to go.'

'That's wonderful,' said Lucy, 'so if you hear Lackey telling Ron to hurt anyone – not just Henry – *anyone*, let me know the details and I'll make sure that he can't do it.'

'Why not stop him doing *anything*?' asked Ben. 'He was talking about making cars not start and stealing sports bags and stuff so that teams would lose matches.'

'I've been thinking about that,' said Lucy. 'As long as we stop him actually *hurting* anyone it might be best to let him do some of the other things.' Ben looked puzzled.

'Why?'

'Because if the elfsibs record some of the conversations between Lackey and Ron Pollard we will have concrete evidence that they actually did things that altered the outcome of games. I know it's hard on the victims, but a few lost football boots or missed trains are not that important when you remember that we are going to send these wicked men to jail and stop them stealing millions of pounds and hurting other people in the future.'

And so it was agreed. Alfie and his elfsibs spent the next week in Z-man's office and when he invited the Gormless boys in, the conversation was recorded. Another set of elves monitored Lackey's office and recorded any conversations he had with Pollard. Fortunately there were no instructions to hurt anyone so Lucy and Grace weren't required to send their animal squads into action.

As it happened, the instructions for the next few months were for St Luigi's to win all their matches. All the scores were specified but Henry didn't care about the scores: he knew that as soon as he had scored enough, then Z-man would pull him out onto the bench and Wayne and Darren would make sure the game ended with the correct score.

As for the teams they played, there seemed to be a succession of extraordinary problems with their strikers and goalies. Stories of stolen football boots, stolen bikes, family cars unable to start on the day of the match, mysterious delays on buses and trains all ensured that St. Luigi's were never in doubt of winning any of their matches. Ron and his team were obviously hard at work.

10

The Great Petnap Mystery

Pets had first been reported missing in February, but as the problem increased and received more publicity, many owners came forward with stories that they had lost pets earlier, in December and January. It started with cats which simply went out and never came back, then dogs – but never when their owner could see them. A dog might chase a ball into some bushes or woodland and not return. Some owners spent hours searching and calling for their beloved pets – but always in vain. At first it was thought that perhaps some wild animal such as a panther might have escaped from a zoo. One owner fancied she had fleetingly seen a large feline shape stalking through the trees on Wimbledon Common and for some weeks there was talk in the local newspapers and pubs about the "Beast of Wimbledon". There were no further sightings, however, and the theory collapsed very quickly when people noticed that dogs were also disappearing when they had been left tied up in gardens or outside shops (usually shops near parks or open countryside). In these cases the leads or chains hadn't been bitten through or broken – they had been *untied*. Suspicion then immediately fell upon an individual or a gang (the latter seemed more probable in view of the sheer scale of the problem) who were stealing the animals to resell as pets elsewhere in the country or abroad, or to sell them to shady restaurants to be served in kebabs, burgers or meat pies.

After a few weeks it became apparent that all the disappearances were occurring within approximately five miles of Wimbledon Common. There were thousands of messages on Twitter and Facebook from worried owners.

Things took a more sinister turn when animals began to disappear from houses in which windows had been left open. Householders might leave a small fanlight window ajar to air a room while they were in a different part of the house. On their return a pet might have disappeared from the room. And not just a cat or a dog. Hamsters, budgies and even goldfish all disappeared. In many cases the birdcage or fish tank would have been taken as well, and then be found empty at the end of the garden. Rabbits and guinea pigs in outdoor hutches disappeared overnight, the hutches remaining intact with their doors shut and locked the following morning.

Then there was a truly astonishing development. A CCTV camera outside a shop showed a large bulldog being chained up by its owner to a purpose-built post provided by the shop, complete with a bowl of water nearby. A few moments after the owner had gone into the shop the chain seemed to work loose and the dog walked away. Some experts viewing the footage maintained that the chain was trailing on the ground – others *that it seemed to remain clear of the ground*. The actual process of the chain working its way loose from the post was observed in its entirety on camera and what was not in doubt was that nobody had come near. The chain was subsequently found about 50 yards away, unfortunately beyond the range of the CCTV, having apparently also worked its way loose from around the dog's neck. The CCTV sequence was reproduced thousands of times on the Internet and even on the national TV news, but experts were unable to agree on precisely what had happened. The bulldog was never seen again. The owner, when interviewed, couldn't understand how any stranger could possibly have taken the dog.

'He wasn't a very ... *sociable* dog,' he explained, when interviewed by a Wimbledon Gazette reporter.

'Would you call him unfriendly?' asked the reporter.

'Well ... yes,' said the owner.

'Well, just how unfriendly was he?' persisted the reporter.

'OK, I'll spell it out,' said the owner. 'If anyone had come too near he would have bitten their arm off.'

And so the mystery deepened. By late March pet owners in the danger zone barely let their pets out of their sight. Most animals now slept in their owners' bedrooms, and cats, kept indoors for days on end, were scratching chairs and beds to bits in their frustration. The 'Missing Pets Mystery' was discussed daily in the media but nobody, despite several forensic investigations by the police and veterinary authorities, was any nearer to a solution. It was now impossible to insure a pet anywhere in South West London and neighbouring Surrey. Those who had lost pets were distraught – many inconsolable in the light of the circumstances in which they had gone missing and the complete uncertainty concerning their fate.

And so the fear and the mystery remained.

Lucy, in common with everyone in the locality, was fully aware of the mystery of the missing pets but things took a personal turn when the next-door cat disappeared. He was a ginger tom. He knew Tibbles, of course, and they did not fight, but regarded each other with deep suspicion and avoided meeting whenever possible. As soon as she heard the news from their tearful neighbour Lucy asked Tibbles if she knew what had happened to him. Tibbles, somewhat to her surprise, said she had heard of other disappearances, and that the animals thought it might be something to do with the invisible creatures of the woods – the creatures that Lucy had asked her about a few days ago. Once again, Tibbles said that Lucy should talk to the clever animals to find out more.

'This settles it,' said Lucy to Grace and Sarah after recounting this conversation to them. 'We've *got* to go and talk to some intelligent animals about the elves; there's obviously something very strange going on.' The others agreed.

'Will we have to go up to London Zoo?' asked Grace. 'I don't expect they've got any bonobos but there are bound to be some ordinary chimpanzees we could talk to.'

'But it's up in north London so they might not know about the missing pets,' said Sarah.

'Good point,' said Lucy. 'Let's ask Tibbles.' She called the cat and asked her which animals might know about the missing pets.

'It is said that there are great creatures who know of many mysteries that other animals do not understand,' said Tibbles. *'They are kept in houses of iron but a league from here – over whence the Brilliant One shines best. They are the ones to whom thou shouldst speak.'*

'Of course!' Lucy exclaimed. She told Sarah what the cat had said and she immediately grinned and nodded. Lucy looked at Grace. 'Do you know what Tibbles is talking about?' Grace looked puzzled.

'Some kind of local zoo to the south?'

'Yes, it's called the Chessington World of Adventures Resort. It's a theme park with lots of rides and it's now fully open again for the summer. Sarah and the cousins love it. But the best thing is – there's a zoo and though it's quite small it's actually got the animals we need for this.'

'Which are?' asked Grace.

'Gorillas!' said Lucy. 'They're the most intelligent animals for miles around. Obviously there are chimps at London Zoo but Chessington's just down the road and they're bound to know about the missing pets. We're incredibly lucky to live so near to animals we can really talk to.'

'We've got an inset day on Wednesday,' said Sarah, 'so we could go and see them then – and as only St Sapientia's will be off that day it means the Zoo will be nice and quiet.'

'Brilliant.' said Lucy. 'I just can't wait to talk to the gorillas and find out what they know.'

'Aren't you forgetting something?' said Grace with a shy smile.

'What?' asked Lucy, puzzled.

'Gorillas are "my" animals.' She put both hands in the air and made a sign for inverted commas with her index and middle fingers.

'O gosh!' said Lucy with a giggle. 'I quite forgot you were – are – queen of the Congo rainforest. OK, you can do the talking and I'll go on Dragon's Fury with Sarah.'

'What's that?' asked Grace.

'Oh, it's a roller-coaster,' said Sarah. 'Terrifying, but great fun. You'll love it!'

'Well let's *all* go to the gorillas first, then all go to the rides – I don't want to miss out on that. Remember I've never been to an adventure park before.'

And so it was agreed.

11

Grilling Gorillas

day dawned bright and clear and the three girls got to the theme park as soon as it opened. They went straight to the zoo which, as they had hoped, was virtually empty of visitors. The gorillas were all standing at the front of their enclosure straining to look for the girls as they came into sight. As they drew near Lucy and Sarah went over to see the tigers and lions so that Grace could speak to the great primates on her own.

'*Greetings, O Promised One,*' said the big male. The female was very shy but Grace could sense her pleasure at meeting her. Two small gorillas were frantic with excitement and reached out to try and clutch at her skirt but were stopped by the reinforced glass. Embarrassed by their mistake, they retreated to admire her from a nearby branch.

'*Greetings to you all, O Great Ones of the forest,*' said Grace. '*Not three moons ago I dwelt with the bonobokin in the Great Forest that is ruled by thine own kin. I was born in that forest and have spoken many times with thy cousins in that far-off land where the Brilliant One is strong.*'

'Greetings to you all,
O Great Ones of the forest...'

'*We were expecting thee,*' continued the male. '*The fledgiquills told us of thy journey hence and we hoped against hope that it was us that thou sought. Our young ones will tell their children's children of this day.*' Grace smiled and waved to the little ones. '*I was born in this very place,*' the gorilla continued, '*but my mother came from the Great Forest. She told me that the animals there had been expecting you since ever any of our kin could remember. She would have never believed that I and my family – her* grandkin *– would actually see you here in this land far from the Great Forest. We are honoured beyond words.*' He paused as if slightly embarrassed. '*But what of the other? I feel her beacon – it is as strong as thine.*'

Grace suddenly remembered Lucy and Sarah.

'*My sisterkin are here. The one whose beacon thou canst feel is my twin. She talks to the stripedfang and the spotfang but I call her now.*' Grace directed her own thoughts to Lucy and there was an immediate response. Soon Lucy was talking to the gorillas and Sarah made funny faces through the glass to the little ones who squealed in delight and tried to copy her.

'*And now,*' said Grace, eventually, '*we seek knowledge that perhaps only you can give us. Tibbles, our furriclaws, says it is beyond her understanding but that you may help us.*'

'*Ask and we shall try to answer.*' He paused and looked fondly at the female. '*My mate speaks but little – especially to such as thee – but understands many things that I find difficult. She may answer you if I cannot.*' Grace and Lucy were astonished and touched that this massive creature, the very embodiment of the alpha male, should pay such a courtesy to his companion.

'What knowledge dost thou seek?'

'Our youngest cousinkin has discovered that he has power to speak to those other than the Tailless Ones – as do we two. But his power has revealed to him tiny tailless ones called the Littlefolk. They are themselves possessed of great powers and we can neither see them nor hear them. Knowest thou of such creatures?'

'Indeed we do,' said the gorilla, *'but …'* he looked for help to the female who came forward shyly to the glass.

'We call these creatures the Wraithkin,' she said quietly, *'though the lesser animals call them the Hiddenkin.'* Lucy suppressed a smile. She certainly wouldn't tell Tibbles this. *'There are many different kinds in this place,'* the gorilla continued, *'and my mother told me of even different ones again in the Great Forest of my forekin. We can smell them, which is how we know they are there and how we know there are different kinds – each has a different scent. They never show themselves, however, and they speak not the common tongue – not, at least, to us. My mother, however, said that once her mother glimpsed these creatures dancing in the light of the Great Silver One and others say they have also seen them on rare occasions. They are indeed just like tiny tailless ones – without fur such as thee and thy kin. Some are said to be a larger kind, less fair of face and these are greatly feared by smaller animals for they are clever hunters from whom no escape is possible. They use their … their …'* she stopped.

'Magic power?' said Grace.

'… if that is power beyond all understanding then that is so. They use their magic power *to capture and kill their prey. They hunt the dreykin, the coneyhops, the hedgiquill and all manner of scurripods.'*

'Come, on you guys!' said Sarah, goodnaturedly. She had been waiting patiently as her sisters stood communicating in silence with the animals. 'What are they saying?'

'Sorry!' said Lucy. 'We were just fascinated. The animals do know about these Littlefolk. They seem to know there are different ones – I suppose they mean goblins and elves and pixies and fairies and such like. A few animals have seen some of them which sound like elves or fairies but only very rarely. Some of the bigger ones – she didn't say how they *knew* they were bigger – actually kill small animals for food. Oh, and they don't speak to the animals – though I suppose we knew that already; otherwise Lucy and I could speak more easily to Alfie.'

'I wonder what these bigger ones are,' said Sarah, intrigued. 'Maybe they're leprechauns or gnomes or something – they're supposed to be bigger than elves and fairies and sprites aren't they?' She paused. 'Ask them how they *know* they're bigger if they can't see them?' Her sisters grinned and turned back to the gorillas. A moment later Lucy spoke to Sarah again. She was smiling.

'They say they *smell* bigger,' she said.

'Well, I know that seems funny to us,' said Sarah, 'but I suppose a lion would smell bigger than a mouse wouldn't it? Especially if you were good at smelling things.'

'Maybe,' said Lucy, 'I don't suppose we'll ever know for certain.' She then asked the gorillas if they had heard anything about the missing pets through the animanet and was fascinated by what she heard. She had just finished recounting this to Sarah when a family approached and three young children hurried up to get as close to the gorillas as they could.

'Time to go,' said Lucy. 'I think we've found out as much as we can. Let's go and try out the Dragon's Fury – though I'd like to try Rameses Revenge afterwards.'

'Huh!' said Sarah. 'You mean the one you were too scared to go on last time!'

They all laughed then Grace and Lucy thanked the gorillas and waved to the little ones who waved back – to the great astonishment of the family who had just arrived. Lucy paused to ask the gorillas also to wave to the new children and then the three sisters went off to introduce Grace to the terrifying and exhilarating pleasures of the theme park.

12

Goblin Gold

The next weekend the cousins met up once again at Lucy's request.

'I've got something serious to discuss,' she started. 'You know the problem of the missing pets is getting worse and worse?' They all nodded; the local papers talked about it every week and there had been articles in the national press and on radio and TV.

'Well I talked to Tibbles about this and she said it was too complicated for her to understand or explain and that I should talk to the gorillas at Chessington World of Adventures. So Grace and Sarah and I went there on our inset day last week.'

'What did they say?' asked Christopher. He was fascinated. He loved the gorillas and always went to see them before going on the rides. The thought that Lucy could actually speak to them was really exciting.

'It was very interesting,' replied Lucy. 'I half thought that they wouldn't know anything about it, but they did – in fact they said all the zoo animals were talking about it and hoping they would be safe in their cages – especially the smaller animals. Anyway, there's something really odd about this and that's why I need you, Christopher.' Christopher looked surprised.

'Me? What can I do?'

'The apes have heard lots of stories from rats and birds who have told them that several animals have *nearly* been caught but have actually escaped. We of course didn't know that – nor did the press – because an owner doesn't know if a pet has had a near miss or not, but if you think about it it's obvious that this must have happened to lots of pets. Well the animals who have had a narrow escape all say the same thing – that there was an incredibly strong scent of one of the ...' she paused, trying to remember the names of the various magical creatures Christopher had described to her, '... one of the *Littlefolk* in the area. Do you think Alfie would know anything about this?'

'I'll ask him,' said Christopher.

'What – now?'

'Why not? I can't wait to hear what he says.'

'Shall we all come?'

'No, I can handle this myself.' The others smiled at each other as he rushed out and disappeared down the garden. He was gone for what seemed like an age to the others but eventually reappeared looking very excited.

'You're not going to believe this,' he said. He paused. 'And I don't really know where to begin.'

'Well just start,' said Lucy kindly, 'and I expect we'll make sense of it as you go along. Are the *elves* stealing the pets?'

'Oh no,' said Christopher. 'It's goblins.'

'Goblins!' the others all chorused.

'Yes, didn't I tell you about goblins? Alfie says there are only about ten goblin clans in the country – which includes everywhere up to the sea all round so it's Wales and Scotland as well. Most of the places they live are very old and hidden away deep in the countryside or woods or mountains – Alfie calls them gobblehides. The nearest one to us is on Wimbledon Common. Like all the others it's been there for thousands of years. Alfie says that the fairies (who know everything) say that the goblins lived in their gobblehides before the Greatfolk came – that's us humans. When people settled in London and London gradually got bigger the humans got nearer and nearer to the gobblehide but the goblins didn't mind. They were invisible to the Greatfolk and the good thing was the gold.'

'Gold?' said Henry.

'Yes, gold. Apparently goblins love gold – in fact they are obsessed with it and there's a massive hoard on the common. In the olden days they used to find nuggets in streams or steal it off the dwarves who dug it out of mines. But then when humans came to live near them they stole it from them. There were old settlements and forts on Wimbledon Common and people were always fighting. The goblins took the gold rings and bracelets off the dead and they also knew where people had buried treasure to keep it safe – as they thought. They also stole gold from houses and picked up lost rings and brooches and stuff.

Alfie says that no-one has ever found anything they lost on the Common – even if they went back to look for it just after they dropped it.'

'That's weird,' said Lucy. 'I've just read an article about that in the Wimbledon Gazette. At the end of yet another story about a missing pet the journalist said that the pets were unlikely to be found because there was an old local legend that anything lost on the common would never be found again. I didn't believe it when I read it, but now we know it must be true!'

'What's all this got to do with the pets?' asked Ben.

'Well,' said Christopher, 'everything was OK until recently. People invented stuff like cars and telephones and radio and TV but it didn't affect the goblins. They stayed invisible and protected their gobblehide by magic. People and animals just can't see it. It's a cave in the woods, quite near one of the main paths on the common, and that cave leads to more caves underground where they store their gold and other treasure.' He stopped for breath and took a swig of his drink. The cousins sat in amazement. The story they were listening to seemed like a fairy tale, literally, but they knew it was true: an elf sitting at the end of the garden in his surreal outfit had just told their cousin this incredible story.

'Anyway,' he continued, 'one day a few years ago a goblin was sitting, invisible to all but the Littlefolk, on a log near the windmill.' They all nodded; they knew the place well. 'Some elves were there, some brownies, a fairy and a couple of dry..dy….'

'Dryads – wood elves?' asked Lucy.

'That's it! Dryads. Well, all the elves and brownies kept away from the goblin – they're much bigger than elves and very aggressive, Alfie says. A man came along with a dog and in his hand he had a mobile phone. Alfie says it was much bigger than yours, Ben.'

'The old ones were enormous,' said Lucy. 'Grandpa says his was like a brick.'

'Anyway, the phone rang and the man touched a switch on it. The elves were OK but the goblin just keeled over and died. Right there. Just rolled off the log. All the elves and other small creatures were OK and didn't know what the problem was. The thing is, Alfie says, Littlefolk never just die, like we do. They can get *killed* but they don't get ill or old. So something killed this goblin. Well soon, Alfie says, all the Littlefolk realised it was mobile phones. When they are being used any goblin nearby gets killed and ones further away get this terrible feeling. Alfie couldn't describe it, he's seen a few goblins suffering from it, but I think it must be like an electric shock. Out of all the Littlefolk it's only the goblins who are affected.'

'Wow,' said Lucy. 'It must be a certain transmission frequency that affects goblin brains or metabolism. But where do the pets come in?'

'I'm coming to that next. Soon there were so many people with mobiles around all the time that the goblins couldn't go near any of their usual places on the common. As you know there are people walking and cycling all over the place: dogwalkers, families, joggers, golfers – and

'The elves were OK, but the Goblin just keeled over and died. Right there. Just rolled off the log...'

they've all got mobiles. Now the problem is that goblins have to eat fresh meat every day – *every* day.'

'But I thought you said they didn't get ill and die,' interrupted Henry.

'That's just what I said to Alfie,' said Christopher. 'They don't just *die*. What happens if they don't eat meat is that they stop being invisible and lose their magic powers – just as Elfie says he has to eat primroses to stay invisible.' The others didn't know this about the elves but they didn't interrupt. 'Then they can get *killed* by anything big enough.' Christopher continued. 'People in the past who said they'd seen a goblin must've just seen one who hadn't been able to get fresh meat for some reason. So now the goblins have a big problem. They usually catch small animals by day but now only the bravest dare come out for fear of somebody appearing with a mobile phone. Most of them stay in the gobblehide.'

'Can't they come out at night?' said Henry.

'They can – I asked that too – but they enjoy the daylight and love the warmth of the sun. But more importantly the *hob*goblins come out at night: it seems that they are bigger and nastier than the goblins and their magic is more powerful. In fact only the fairies have greater powers. There are two hobblehides nearby, one in Richmond Park and one on Coombe Hill. At night the hobgoblins cross that big road …'

'The A3,' said Lucy.

'Whatever,' said Christopher. 'They cross that and hunt all night on Wimbledon Common. Any goblins they see they kill or capture as slaves. The goblins have become so desperate for fresh meat that they have even started to eat elves and sprites and brownies – even though that is forbidden under the Ancient Code – that's why Alfie was attacked. Alfie thinks that particular goblin was a brave one who came out for meat during the day and was hunting on the golf course near our house where mobiles aren't allowed. He saw Alfie – and well you know what happened.'

'So, what about the *pets*?' said Ben again, and everybody laughed.

'I really am coming to that now,' said Christopher. 'Because the goblins are trapped they have declared war on the Greatfolk. They can't harm them – that's also against the Ancient Code but they think that the humans have to have pets near them and if they take away the pets, the humans will go away.'

'But that's so stupid,' said Henry. 'People don't *need* pets and anyway they won't go away.'

'I know,' said Christopher. '*We* all know. And the elves know. But the goblins don't know. Alfie says the goblins are stupid. Like *really* stupid. They think if they take our pets we'll go away with our mobiles and leave them in peace.'

'I feel a bit sorry for them,' said Sarah. 'It's not their fault that our mobiles hurt them and they've lived here for ages – longer than *we* have according to Alfie.'

The others thought about what she had said. It was true.

'Well, at least we know what's happening,' said Lucy, '– even though we can't tell anyone: it's a feeling I've had to get used to in the last few years. But this is so important I think it would be helpful if we *all* talked to Alfie. We may find out more with different people asking questions. Is that OK Christie?'

'Of course,' he replied. 'I was just telling you what he told me. When I went out I'd no idea he was going to tell me all this stuff, but it would be great to find out more.' They all trooped down the garden to find Alfie.

'I've been telling the others what you told me,' said Christopher, 'and they're really interested. Can you tell them any more about the goblins and the mobiles?'

'Of course,' replied the elf. 'It's really very simple. It is impossible for me to exaggerate how much the goblins fear these mobile phone machines. In order to catch the pets they sometimes have to go quite near the greatfolk who might switch on their phone at any moment. Only the very bravest of goblins undertake this work and they are much admired by the others for the risks they take – many, indeed have died or suffered dreadful agonies from their attempts.'

'So they are like commandos – special soldiers – for the goblins,' said Sarah.

'Exactly,' agreed the elf. 'They are willing to take these risks to save their clan from extermination.'

'And the pets they catch, are they ... *eating* them?' asked Christopher, not sure if he wanted to hear the answer.

'At first they didn't,' replied the elf, 'The fairies strongly disapprove of them eating animals so closely linked to the Greatfolk. Rabbits and rodents are their favourite foods – oh, and snakes of course. Snakes can't see them but seem fascinated by their scent: they must think goblins are a new kind of rodent and follow them into their gobblehides. They don't last long – goblins are even faster than they are and they paralyse their prey with ancient magic.'

'So, if they don't kill the pets what happens to them?' asked Lucy.

'Ah, that's a kind of cruel goblin joke,' said the elf. They turn the dogs into cats and the cats into birds or mice. So the animals become one of the species that they have chased or hunted or killed during their lives – sort of getting a taste of their own medicine. Then they let them go. It is said that many of these poor creatures eventually find their way home – especially the birds but, of course, their owners don't recognise them.'

'How awful,' said Christopher. Then he remembered how the elf had first answered his question.

'You said that the goblins didn't eat the pets *at first*,' he said nervously. 'What … what are they doing now?'

'I'm afraid …' said the elf, somewhat hesitantly. He glanced sideways at Sarah for he knew she had a cat, ' … that as they have grown more desperate for fresh meat, they are now eating more and more of the pets they catch Even though the fairies don't like it they realize that the goblins really don't have any choice if they are to survive. It has, of course, become even worse for the goblins because it is now much harder for them to steal pets. The Greatfolk know that their animals are in danger and are taking much greater care of them. And when they are out with their dogs they try always to keep them nearby or in sight which means that the goblins are in even greater danger from the mobiles.' There was silence as they all reflected on what Alfie had told them.

'Thank you for explaining everything,' said Lucy, eventually. 'The situation is obviously getting desperate for both the goblins and the pet owners so we've got to do something – and quickly! Let's all go home and think of what we can do.' They all said goodbye to Alfie who, as was now his custom, hovered in front of each of them in turn to shake one of their fingers, and then they all dispersed – each reluctant later to wash the finger that had been brushed with elven gold.

13

Perplexing Pets

THE WIMBLEDON GAZETTE
(Thursday 3rd March)
A Pet Mystery
by Petula Paucity, our domestic affairs correspondent

As if the horrifying spate of pet disappearances were not enough of a mystery, Mrs Gloria Pethasgone of Copse Hill told me about the extraordinary events in her home this week. One week ago Gloria's cat Tilly went out after her morning sleep. She normally returns without fail for her evening meal but did not reappear and her whereabouts remain unknown. The day after her disappearance Gloria heard a tapping on the cat flap. Puzzled, she went to investigate and to her astonishment found a wood pigeon sitting outside the back door. It seems the bird had been pecking at the cat-flap . Instead of flying away the bird hopped over the back step, walked into the kitchen and went straight over to the cat's food bowl. The pigeon pecked perfunctorily at some of the food in the bowl but then turned and looked expectantly at Gloria. Intrigued,

Gloria put down a bowl of the seed she used in her garden birdfeeder and the pigeon immediately gobbled it up. It then waddled unhesitatingly across the kitchen to the cat's basket, Gloria watched in a state of growing disbelief as – prepare yourself, dear reader, for a shock – the pigeon plumped the cushion in the cat's basket with its feet, turned round two or three times and sat down in the basket as though hatching eggs in a nest.

Just after Gloria had told me this story there was a tapping on the door of the breakfast room where we were sitting.

'What on earth is that?' I asked, slightly worried for I had thought we were alone in the house. Gloria smiled.

'Oh, didn't I mention that the pigeon is having a little roost in Tilly's basket at the moment? It must be ready for an outing.' She opened the door and to my utter amazement a pigeon strutted in. It gave me a passing disdainful glance, flew up onto the windowsill, and waited until Gloria opened the window. It then flew off. Gloria turned to me with a smile.

'It'll be back later for food,' she said. 'It seems to think it lives here now.'

I commented to Gloria on the bird's rather unusual black and white markings – its colouring was more like a magpie than a pigeon.

'That's the really spooky thing,' she said. 'I know it sounds crazy, comparing a cat and a bird, but those marking are identical to Tilly's.' She paused and picked up her phone. 'Look at these photos! That's Tilly,' she

'...the pigeon...sat down in the basket as though hatching eggs in a nest.'

said, 'and this is one I took of the pigeon this morning. Amazing isn't it?' It certainly was amazing. It was as if a computer program had been used to transform the cat into a bird with identical markings. 'Just look at the pigeon's feet,' said Gloria. 'Tilly has two black front paws and on her hind paws she has black toes on her right foot and white on her left.'

I looked and there, instead of the usual reddish feet and toes of a pigeon, was a black right foot and a white left foot: even more striking was the fact that the tips of both wings were jet black!

Now if you think that we at the Gazette have been spending too much time at the Cat and Fox, I should tell you something else. Since my interview with Gloria three days ago we have had no fewer than five calls from pet owners who have recently lost pets in the Wimbledon area and who have been experiencing some unusual experiences with strange animals. I will be interviewing these callers in the next few days and hope to come back to you with some further fascinating and mysterious stories.

THE WIMBLEDON GAZETTE
(Thursday 17th March)
The ongoing pet mystery
by Petula Paucity, our domestic affairs correspondent

A fortnight ago in this column I reported my extraordinary interview with Mrs Gloria Pethasgone about a pigeon *which seems to have adopted her since her cat went missing on the Common. A pigeon, moreover, which has apparently identical markings to her cat. I can now report on an even more mystifying case of a dog replaced by a cat. Liz Canamans was utterly devastated by the disappearance of her King Charles spaniel, Lassie, three weeks ago while she was walking near Caesar's Camp on the Common. She had a merciful distraction from her loss by the curious behaviour of a cat who appeared in her house about a week after Lassie went missing.*

'First thing that morning I was just putting the kettle on when I heard the dog flap clunk' Liz told me when I interviewed her in her home today in Cannizaro Road. 'For a second or two I thought it was Lassie coming in – she used to go and sniff round the garden before breakfast – then I remembered the horrible truth: Lassie was gone. I spun round and to my utter astonishment there was a cat standing looking at me. It was not one of our neighbourhood cats: I know them all well even though they kept well clear of Lassie: she was a pathological cat-hater I'm afraid. I'd never set eyes on this one before. The extraordinary thing – unbelievable really – is that this cat had identical markings to Lassie! I was so astonished I took a picture, look!' Liz broke off to show me a picture on her phone and then showed me a framed photograph of Lassie on the kitchen cabinet. The cat on the phone had identical markings to the King Charles spaniel in the photograph, even down to the smallest details such as a Blenheim spot in the middle of her forehead. I was

stupefied at the similarity of the animals' colouration. Before I could comment, Liz continued.

'But that's not the only thing. The really spooky thing is that after looking at me, the cat went through to the breakfast room and straight to the corner where we used to put Lassie's food. It wasn't there, of course. I had left it there just in case Lassie returned or someone found her, but after a few days I found it so upsetting that I cleared her bowls away and asked the cleaner to give that corner a good scrubbing when she did the floor. How did the cat know where Lassie's bowl should have been? Anyway, I gave her some dog food in Lassie's bowl and she gobbled it up. By now the children had come down for breakfast and were very excited to see our new arrival, who actually broke off from eating, started to wag her tail – not swishing it like a cross cat but wagging it – and then went over to paw Holly and Zac in turn and lick their hands. Can you believe it? Then, when she'd finished a second helping of food, she stretched, walked into the hall and stood by the living room door. I just had to see what she wanted so I opened it and she hurried over to the corner where Lassie's basket used to be. Then – and this I can hardly believe – then she went out of the living room, upstairs and into our bedroom. She walked over to the corner where the sun shines in the morning and where Lassie loved to curl up and snooze if she could sneak in when the door was open. She looked at me as if to say "don't chuck me out today," lay down and went to sleep.'

Well, readers, you might think that Liz is suffering from the shock of losing her beloved Lassie and is imagining this story (she has, incidentally, seen this article and given full permission to the Gazette to publish it). There are a couple of twists to this tale, however, that I need to share with you. First of all, when I had finished my interview with Liz she said:

'I expect you think I've gone a bit barmy after losing Lassie – which is quite understandable. So I'd like you to watch this, if you can spare another minute.'

Intrigued, I watched as she went to the window and opened it.

'Lassie!' she called. 'Lassie come on. Good girl!' She closed the window. A moment or two later the dog-flap clunked and the cat came in. As I watched in open amazement Liz then said:

'Walkies?' The cat purred, wagged its tail and skipped around and then went to a hook on the wall and clawed at a leash and collar that were hanging there.

'We're going out now for a walk,' Gloria told me. 'We do this every day but I don't let her off the leash on the Common – I'm not going to lose another dear friend.'

I thanked Liz for her time and stumbled speechless to my car. I have no idea what is going on, but it seems beyond coincidence that at least two pet owners – and I am due to interview several more – have been visited by previously unknown animals after losing their own pets – animals which not only seem to know the geography of the owner's house but have the same colouration *as the missing pets. If anyone knows what is going on please let me know. We would particularly welcome any information from veterinary surgeons or animal behavioural psychologists who have any theories about these phenomena or, indeed, have had any previous experience of such events.*

THE WIMBLEDON GAZETTE
(Thursday 31st March)
Even more pet puzzles
by Petula Paucity, our domestic affairs correspondent

Following my two previous articles in this column on curious animal behaviour I have received a deluge of further reports on the same theme. A common feature of all of these is that these bizarre occurrences have only *affected householders who lost pets in the ongoing petnapping spate. While earlier examples concerned strange birds and cats – around two dozen of these have now come to my attention, and they continue to occur – a group of more recent stories come from houses only in very close proximity to the Common. These relate to visits by* mice *which seem almost totally unafraid of humans and have markings not commonly observed in mice: several animals have been black and white, several have been ginger and at least three have had tabby-like markings. The further bizarre feature is one I hesitate to report, as we have reached the end of the month, for fear of being accused of preparing an elaborate April Fool joke. I do suspect, though, that those of you who have been following this column in recent weeks have already guessed what I am about to say: Each mouse appearing at one of these households* has had identical markings to the owners' missing pets! *There seems to be something going on here that is completely beyond my comprehension. In my thirty years of reporting for this newspaper I have never come across a mystery as impenetrable and intriguing as this one.*

One of the country's most eminent psychiatrists has suggested that the householders concerned, all deeply traumatised by the recent loss of a dear pet, and many of whom are communicating on Twitter and Facebook, may in fact be exhibiting what is known as mass psychosis. While I, as a humble reporter, would not question this professional view, I feel I have to report that in the last week I have personally seen a ginger ring-necked parakeet, a Dalmatian cat, a Siamese mouse and several tabby mice. Maybe I have a journalistic psychosis?

14

A Match to Remember!

And now it came to the final stages of the under-elevens league. St Luigi's and Ingots had accumulated an equal number of points so Ron had obviously been making sure that Ingots' opponents were incapable of winning. The final was to be played on the last Saturday of April and on the previous Monday Alfie reported to Christopher that Lackey had told Pollard that Henry was not to attend the match under any circumstances – Pollard was to do *anything* necessary to stop him. Alfie said that on the same day his other elfsibs had heard Mr Z telling the Gormless twins that they were to lose the match against Ingots and that they would receive a special bonus for doing so.

As soon as Christopher had told his brothers Ben rang Lucy with the news.

'OK,' she said calmly. 'Tell Henry not to worry and carry on as usual. Nothing – *nothing* – bad is going to happen to him. I'm going straight into action so tell him not to be surprised if you see some unusual animals hanging around. They'll protect him 24/7.' Ben told the others, and even as he finished speaking a flock of vicious-looking crows flew into the garden and positioned themselves on trees and fences around the garden. A little while later some red kites appeared high above their house and circled lazily above on the wind currents on their giant wings, their fantastic eyesight enabling them to scan everything that moved in the entire surrounding area.

'See,' said Ben, 'Lucy's already got her troops in position – and if anything gets past the birds she'll get some dogs on the case. I saw her do some incredible things in Africa with leopards and snakes and stuff – Oh and she told me she's going to stop Pollard leaving his house until the game's over on Saturday!'

Henry was very relieved as he looked in amazement at the birds sent to guard him.

'It's fantastic we've got her and Alfie looking after us,' he said. 'I don't feel the slightest bit worried any more.'

After the final football practice on Thursday, Henry, Dominic and the Gormless boys were the last ones in the changing room. Henry and Dominic left before Wayne and Darren, but as he went along the corridor Henry suddenly realised he had left his tie behind and ran back. The door was ajar and he heard the twins talking.

'I know the money's useful,' Wayne was saying, 'but I honestly don't want to lose against those stupid Ingots. We beat them last year and we could easily beat them this year – especially with Henry being so good.'

'But you know what Z-man said at lunchtime,' said Darren. 'This is the big one. We've *got* to lose this match; it's the final and he'll give us a special bonus for losing.'

'Huh, even if we try to lose, Henry could still win the match. He's so good he's almost like magic. But I suppose you're right, we'd better throw this one – though I'm telling you now I'm not doing this next year. We've both always wanted to be footballers when we leave school and that won't happen if we go round losing matches.'

Henry coughed and banged the door as he went in and the twins stopped talking. Henry retrieved his tie and turned to go.

'Bye, Henry,' said Wayne. 'Good practice wasn't it?'

'Yeah,' replied Henry. 'See you tomorrow – and don't forget Chelsea are at home to Arsenal tonight!' They waved and he went out and made his way thoughtfully home.

After tea Henry recounted the conversation he had overheard to his brothers. Ben laughed.

'Z-man's going to be desperate that nothing messes up his plans. What a massive shock he's going to get on Saturday!'

'Well, I just hope I play well,' said Henry, 'but at least I'm not worried about Pollard: there's no way he can beat Alfie and Lucy. I still can't believe how quickly she got those birds to come on Monday.'

'Yeah,' said Ben, 'and that is just a *fraction* of what I've seen her do. You're as safe as can be.'

'Anyway,' Henry continued, 'what I'm really interested in is what Wayne said – and they were actually quite nice to me as I left – I forgot to tell you that.' He hesitated. 'If they really are thinking of ditching Z-man do they have to be involved when we give our evidence in?'

Ben thought for a moment.

'No ... oo,' he said. 'We've got Z-man telling Podpilasky and Lackey that he's bribed some of the team but we haven't got *them* on video. And we don't need to show the video we've got of him giving them money. Why?' Henry looked relieved.

'Well, I was thinking that if I told them that somehow we knew about Z-man being a crook and that he's going to get done we might persuade them not to try and lose the final against Ingots. It would be much easier for me to win the game and if Z-man did try to implicate them later, it would be obvious to anyone who watched the match that nobody on our team was trying to lose.'

'Well, I don't mind,' said Christopher. 'I've always been a bit worried about them getting into trouble – especially as football is the only thing they're any good at.'

'Yeah, I agree,' said Ben. 'But how can you tell them we know about Z-man?'

'Simple,' said Henry. 'I'll pretend I overheard Mr Jupiter talking about it to the police on his mobile. I can say he went into the playground at the end of break so his secretary wouldn't hear. Everybody else had gone in to lessons but he didn't realise I was still there doing up my shoelace behind that big tree near the door.' Ben and Christopher both smiled.

'OK,' said Ben.

'OK,' said Christopher.

The next day was Friday, the day before the final and Henry sought out Wayne and Darren at break.

'Listen,' said Henry, cautiously. 'I've got something to ask you guys. Well, something to tell you and then something to ask you.' The twins looked at him, their expressions a mixture of suspicion and curiosity.

'I don't know quite where to start with this,' he continued, 'but you know I'm not stupid and it's pretty obvious that for some time you guys have had it in for me at football and that Z-man has been deliberately ignoring serious fouls.' He stopped to gauge their reaction. Wayne looked uncomfortable; Darren looked truculent.

'So?' said Darren as Henry waited.

'So I think there is something you should know. I overheard something yesterday.' He went on to tell them the story he had agreed with Ben and Christopher. As he spoke various emotions crossed their faces in turn: first disbelief, then shock, then anger and finally, he was encouraged to see, fear. 'Now I don't know what he's got over you two,' he said finally, 'whether he's threatening you or bribing you but you're obviously involved.' There was a long, long silence, eventually broken by Wayne.

'He's paying us.'

'Shurrup Wayne!' said Darren. 'Don't say nothin, *nothin!*'

'He already knows, Darren,' said his brother in a resigned tone. He looked at Henry. 'You do, don't you? I'm right?'

'Yeah,' said Henry. 'The new bikes and phones were pretty obvious clues. But I had to be sure because I wanted to warn you. If – *when* – Z-man goes down you don't want to go down with him. It'll kill your Mum.' It was a penetrating shaft, as Henry had intended it to be.

'You – you leave our Mum out of this,' stuttered Darren, but the fight had gone out of him and his face betrayed his true feelings.

'Listen,' said Henry, 'I know more than you think.' He told them about the conversation he had overheard between Mr Z and Podpilasky and Lackey.

'Wow!' breathed Wayne when Henry had finished. 'That explains Z-man's posh car.'

'And I bet those strange guys I saw after school one day are the ones you've just told us about,' said Darren.

'What if ...' Wayne looked worried '... what if Z-man tries to blame us?'

'If he gets arrested he might,' said Henry truthfully – he had discussed this with the others, 'but that's all the more reason for you not to do what he wants. If you play well he can hardly say he bribed you to lose the match can he? Well he *can*, but nobody will believe him.'

'That's true,' said Darren. 'But I don't want anything to do with the police. My Mum would go mad.' This was just what Henry wanted to hear. He already knew that concern for his mother was Darren's vulnerable point.

'That's right,' he said, 'the best thing you can do is to play well tomorrow and not tell anybody – *anybody* about this.'

'But Z-man is going to be really furious with us,' said Wayne. 'Like *really* furious!'

'I know the feeling,' said Henry with a bitter laugh. 'But I survived …' he paused, then couldn't resist adding '… and I survived you two as well.'

The others looked at each other then both gave Henry a shame-faced grin.

'Yeah,' said Darren. 'We're – like – sorry about that. But – we gotta think about this an' talk about it. So we're not sayin' yes or no now.' He looked enquiringly at his brother who nodded in agreement (somewhat hesitantly, thought Henry).

'But whatever we decide,' said Wayne, 'there'll be no more fouls – that was well out of order.'

That evening, as Jane drew the curtains Ben heard her exclaim in surprise.

'What's up, Mum?' he asked.

'Those dogs.' She pointed into the drive. Three dogs were sitting in the drive near their car. *Big* dogs. 'What on earth are they doing? Do you think I should shoo them away?'

'I should leave them, Mum. They'll go off home soon I expect – and in the meantime they'll keep the foxes away.' Even as he spoke a large bird swooped down and perched on the fence nearest the car.

'Goodness!' said Jane. 'What's going on? That's a barn owl. Here of all places.' She rushed to get her camera, hoping that she'd get something of a picture in the dusk. Ben smiled. As it happened, they were going to the match by public transport tomorrow, but Lucy and Alfie were obviously taking no chances.

The final match of the league was being held at a famous London stadium and the family set off in good time. As they left home Jane was surprised to see some dogs still in the drive and outside on the pavement – different animals from those she had seen the previous evening. As she was discussing this with Marcus two of the largest dogs detached themselves from the group and walked behind the family to the railway station.

'Look at those two!' she said. 'Anyone would think they were accompanying us!' Ben said nothing but smiled to himself. He saw a shadow in the sky and looked up. A red kite soared effortlessly above them in wide circles. Its forked tail twisted delicately to maintain its position in response to every slight change in the wind and its keen eyes scanned the suburban roads and paths in every direction. Its gaze always returned to Henry, his shock of red hair instantly identifiable in the family group. Ben knew its fearsome beak and talons would wreak havoc on any man or beast that threatened Henry and that, if necessary, it would sacrifice its life in his defence. When they reached the station he saw it alight on the sloping roof above the platform where it remained, ever-watchful, until they were safely aboard the train. As the train pulled out of the station the great bird took off once more and, apparently effortlessly, followed the train carrying the one whom it had been charged to protect from all danger.

When they arrived at the great stadium Jane went to their front row seats with Ben and Christopher while Marcus took Henry to join the rest of the school team at the changing room they had been allocated. Mr Z was standing at the door greeting the boys. When he saw Henry and Marcus his face changed and his eyes bulged with surprise.

'Good morning, Mr Z,' said Marcus cheerily – then stopped in concern as he saw the man's expression. 'I say,' he added. 'Are you ... are you feeling OK?'

Mr Z tried to speak but only a croak emerged. He cleared his throat, still staring at Henry as though he were looking at an apparition. Marcus stepped forward and put out a hand to steady him.

'Come and sit down for a minute,' he said kindly, 'you're as white as a sheet.'

Mr Z let himself be led to a bench in the changing room and sat down heavily.

'I'm OK,' he stammered eventually. 'Just came over a bit faint.'

'OK,' said Marcus, looking worried. 'Well ... if you're sure ... I'll go back to the family.' He turned to wish Henry good luck but he had already gone over to join the rest of the team who were busy lacing up their boots.

'Make sure you win!' said Marcus encouragingly to Mr Z as he moved off. He would have been astonished to hear the obscene and venomous answer he received in answer, but was already out of earshot when it was uttered.

As Henry stood in the centre of the pitch, the ball at his feet, he glanced to the touchline and saw Mr Z, his face still seething with rage and bewilderment.

The red kite now circled high overhead and a flock of crows, who had been waiting for the family as they emerged from the underground station, had now settled on the stadium roof surrounding the pitch, looking for all the world like a gallery of avian spectators. Ben had said nothing about the dogs and the birds, but seeing them Henry suddenly realised that they must be something to do with Lucy and felt reassured by their presence. As he glanced over at his family Christopher waved in encouragement and gave him a thumbs-up sign. Mr Z was sitting a few yards away from his family, still pale with anger and fear, and further along the front row were Podpilasky and Lackey, both in hats and dark glasses. Despite his media fame Podpilasky went unrecognised by the other spectators who were all intent on their sons, grandsons and brothers on the pitch.

Henry stood between Wayne and Darren, with Dominic behind in midfield. Henry hadn't dared look at the twins, and was on tenterhooks to know how they were going to play today. There was only one way to find out and when the whistle blew he passed the ball straight to Wayne.

As the opposing striker moved to challenge him, Wayne passed the ball back to Henry, now moving forward fast, and he immediately passed to Darren on his right. As the Ingots' centre midfield moved forward to him Darren passed back to Henry. As he took the ball he felt a thrill of elation – they were obviously playing to win. He skilfully outmanoeuvred the midfielder and the back coming forward from behind him and shot immediately for goal. The ball sped like a bullet and though the keeper reached it there was no way he could stop it: the ball thudded into the net. A goal in under one minute! St Luigi's went wild with joy as Ingots stared in mute disbelief. Henry glanced at Mr Z, now white with fury as he saw, for the first time ever, Wayne and Darren and Henry clustered in a triumphal hug. And so the game went on. Now that Henry had two other helpers in the attack as well as Dominic he passed generously to the others in a way he had not felt it safe to do in previous matches. Goal after goal was scored and by the final minute Wayne and Darren had scored three goals each, Dominic two goals and Henry four goals. Ingots had barely got into St Luigi's half and had scored no goals and had been awarded no corners. Twenty seconds to go and as the Ingots' striker passed to his back-up on the midline, Henry dashed between the two and stole the ball. From the corner of his eye he saw the referee looking at his watch and he thumped the ball as hard as he could. He was fifteen yards from the goal. The ball soared over the heads of the defenders and curved gracefully downwards and inwards to squeeze into the top corner of the goal. The keeper didn't have a chance. Even as the ball rolled to a stop against the back of the net the whistle blew and the St Luigi's spectators erupted into a frenzy of cheering, whistling and shouting. A score of thirteen – nil in the final was unheard of. The team surrounded the three front strikers and hugged and chanted in delight as Henry, Wayne and Darren high-fived each other. The match was won and the day was done.

On the way home the family chatted excitedly about the match and the boys analysed and re-analysed every goal. After tea the boys went into the garden to see Alfie. Henry had been getting progressively more subdued since the match and Ben asked him what was wrong.

'It's pretty obvious isn't it?' said Henry, who was now close to tears. 'We won the final and I scored five goals but it wasn't me, was it? It was the elves. And I've been getting all the credit and it makes me feel a bit sick.' Ben stopped and looked at him sympathetically, then gestured to Christopher to go on ahead down the garden while he tried to comfort Henry.

A few moments later they went to join Christopher who was talking to Alfie. The elf was sitting on the wheelbarrow in a St Luigi's strip and as Christopher listened to him a broad smile crossed his face and he turned, delighted, to the others.

'Guess what?' he said. Ben looked puzzled and Henry remained glum and just shrugged his shoulders.

'The elves didn't help Henry at all. In fact they haven't for the last three games. Alfie says that helping him when all this started gave him confidence and I suppose all that messing about and practising that the three of us did with the elves has just given him brilliant ball skills.' Henry, open-mouthed, went and grabbed Christopher.

'You're just saying that Christie – to make me feel good. It's not true!' He punched Christopher in his anger and frustration and knocked him over.

'It's true!' said Christopher, almost in tears. 'It *is* true!' Alfie jumped down and walked over to the centre of the little group, facing Henry as Ben helped Christopher back to his feet.

'It is true,' he said quietly. 'Although we elves are allowed to play tricks we cannot tell a lie under the ancient Fairie Code. In fact there were no elves on the pitch for any of the game today. They were on the touchline and sitting on the goal crossbars to make sure the villains didn't start to do anything desperate when they saw how the match was going. They were also going to intervene in the game if Ingots started fouling or if they thought the referee or the linesmen were deliberately making bad calls. As it happened they didn't need to do anything. You won the match fair and square.' Henry looked chastened but still a little doubtful.

'Well, if that's true, it was the others as well as me,' he said, generously. 'It was nice having Wayne and Darren with me instead of against me for a change.'

'And now I would like to shake your hand and congratulate you.' The elf flew up and hovered in front of Henry. As he hung as though suspended, perfectly motionless in front of Henry in an exquisite demonstration of aerial skill, they could see the pearly opalescence of his wings, iridescent in the evening sunshine, only the merest vibrations hinting at the incredible speed at which they must be beating. Henry felt ashamed as he looked into those clear green eyes and saw that, indeed, they showed nothing but the truth. He held out his little finger and the elf solemnly took it in both hands and shook it. His touch was like the lightest thistledown and when he let go Henry saw that his skin had taken on a golden hue where the magical being had touched him. He turned to Christopher and hugged him.

'Henry felt ashamed as he looked into those clear green eyes'.

'I'm sorry, Christie.' There was nothing more that needed to be said.

'That's OK,' said Christopher. He paused and grinned. 'It was a pathetic little punch anyway – I dived actually.' They all laughed and then the elf flew to Christopher's shoulder and whispered into his ear. Christopher's face was a picture as he listened. First he showed surprise, then comprehension and finally happiness.

'Thank you,' he said eventually, aloud so his brothers could hear. 'Thank you ever so much – and I don't mind if the others know. Can I tell them?' The elf smiled and nodded.

What was all that about? asked Ben.

'It's something nice,' said Christopher. 'He whispered it to me so as not to embarrass me in front of you two. I actually don't mind if you know but it's a bit complicated.'

'Try us – I think we'll manage,' said Ben with a laugh.

'You remember how this all started? – I saved Alfie's life and he granted me a wish.' The others both nodded. 'And you remember that what I wished for was that Henry would get in the team.' They both nodded again and on remembering this Henry felt even guiltier about his recent outburst. 'Anyway,' Christopher continued, 'as you know Alfie rewarded me for...' he blushed slightly, '... well, being generous by helping me with *my* football. What he told me just now was that because I had improved so much – like Henry – he had stopped helping me me too. He hasn't actually helped me in any of my last four games – and, as you know, I was the top scorer in all of them.'

'Well done!' Ben exclaimed and he and Henry gave Christopher a high-five. Then Christopher stopped as the elf spoke.

'What is this with your hands, is it like a handshake?' Christopher laughed.

'Sort of. We do it when we are pleased or have accomplished something good.'

'Can elves do it too?'

'Of course – if you think your hand's big enough, that is!' They all laughed as the elf flew to each of the brothers in turn and, as they each held a palm in the air, they felt the tiniest touch like the brush of a feather as the little creature high-fived them. Later, each of them found a tiny golden patch on his palm.

15

Anonymous Accusations

The next weekend the six cousins held another council of war. Under the pretext of playing Monopoly they discussed what to do next.

'Now the league final's over,' said Ben, 'we've got to decide how to tell the police – or whoever – about Z-man and the other lot.'

'Good,' said Lucy. 'I've had a few ideas about that already.'

'And after that,' said Henry, '*I've* got something to say.' They all looked at each other and laughed.

'OK,' said Lucy. 'You go first, Ben.'

'I don't think we can get involved in any way,' he said. 'It's just too complicated. We might have to give evidence in court and there'll be all kinds of questions. We obviously can't talk about the elves or the animals so some things we say will seem suspicious.'

'So what do we do?' asked Henry with a frown.

'We do it anonymously,' said Sarah.

'Exactly,' said Ben.

'What's anomously?' asked Christie. Lucy smiled kindly and explained.

'So,' Ben continued when she had finished, 'I think we go through all our recordings and select the ones that don't incriminate Wayne and Darren. Then we copy them onto USB sticks. Then we send them anonymously to ... that's what I was wondering ... to just whom *do* we send them? Is it the police or the school or the council or the tax people?'

'I think we send them to several places,' said Lucy. 'Then somebody will have to take action rather than just suppressing it to avoid a fuss. And wherever we send them we include a list of everywhere else they have gone. So, we send them to the police, the school, the football authorities – whatever they're called ...'

'FIFA,' said Ben.

'... and the embassy of whatever country Podpilasky is from.' She paused. 'Anywhere else?'

'Is there some gambling authority?' asked Grace.

'Oh yes, of course there must be – we'll find out what they're called,' said Lucy.

'What about our local MP?' said Sarah.

'Good idea!' said Lucy. 'I'm sure there are other people who'd be interested but that sounds like enough to be going on with. If you sort out the recording stuff, Ben, I'll work out what we're going to say with Grace and Sarah and then we can cut the words out of newspapers ...'

'With gloves on!' said Sarah.

'... yes, with gloves on,' laughed Lucy, 'and make a master letter, and copy it at a copier somewhere in London, not near here, and post it in London with the USBs to all the people we've said – oh and make sure Ben that the copies are also done with gloves on so there are no fingerprints.'

'I know!' said Grace. 'Let's send it to the papers as well. They'll make sure something happens.'

'Of course,' said Lucy. 'Brilliant! Why didn't we think of that before?'

'And we should send it to a local paper as well as a national one,' said Ben.

'This is great,' said Sarah. 'We'll get massive publicity. But we've got to be really careful about covering our tracks. I think we should be OK. We've all seen so many detective series on TV we know about forensics. We'll check with each other exactly what we've done so there are no mistakes. Then we sit back and wait for the fun to start!'

They all laughed. It was an exciting prospect.

'What about Wayne and Darren?' said Christopher. 'I know they're idiots but we don't really want them to get into serious trouble do we? Maybe they'll go to prison.'

Grace calmed him down.

'I'm sure they won't go to prison – they're too young anyway. The police or whoever will say they came under "undue influence from an authority figure" – that's Mr Z – and they'll get let off with a ticking off.' She paused. 'And they may not even be suspects – Ben's told me he's already edited the recordings and video footage so that Wayne and Darren don't feature at all. We'll have enough evidence from the conversations between Z-man and the baddies to incriminate them without the boys ever being mentioned.'

'OK, that's settled,' said Lucy. 'We'll all get on with the things we've said and then have a final meeting before we post the stuff. Now, what was the other thing *you* wanted to say, Henry?'

'I've been wondering about us and Dominic and the twins,' said Henry. 'I've been thinking about next year when we've all left St Luigi's. Ben and Sarah are already at secondary schools where the football seems OK but not brilliant. When Z-man leaves – as I expect he will have to if our plan succeeds – football isn't going to be as good at St Luigi's. Whatever else he is, he's a fantastic PE teacher and that means the football probably won't be so good for Christie at school.'

'What are you saying?' asked Sarah.

'Well I'm just wondering whether we should start a football club. We could all still play together then on Saturdays and when we start to play other teams the elves can help us – not to cheat of course, but to make sure other teams don't foul us and to put things right if there are bad decisions by the referee. I know they don't owe us any favours any more but they seem to like having something to do and they certainly enjoy the football.'

'Wouldn't we have to get a pitch to play on?' said Christopher.

'Yes,' said Henry, 'there'll be loads of stuff to organise, but we can do it if everyone wants to.'

'I think it's a *great* idea,' said Sarah. 'Let's try it – if it doesn't work we can always stop.'

'What will you call yourselves?' asked Lucy with a grin, '"The Ever-hopefuls"?'

'No,' said Ben. 'How about "The Elven Rovers"'.

'Brilliant!' said Henry. And so they agreed to make some plans and Henry said he would talk to Dominic and the twins.

Ron's mobile phone rang with his usual ring tone – Chopin's Death March.

'Wot?' he snarled.

'This is Podpilasky,' was the reply. 'What the hell are you playing at? That red-haired kid was meant to be dealt with today but there he was, large as life, winning the match. Cost me millions.'

'Not my fault, boss,' said Ron. 'I couldn't get near my car because of some vicious dogs and anyway I could see every tyre had been let down. I rang for a taxi but the dogs wouldn't let me get out of the gate. I rang Lennie and Sean but they had a dog problem as well, somethin' really weird is goin' on.'

'Well as soon as you pluck up the courage to say boo to a couple of dogs you can get round to Zdradzacski's place and take the car back. We'll leave Zdradzacski himself until I've thought of something – something slow, painful and fatal. Now get moving!'

Ron looked out at the three Rottweilers padding round his car and the Pit Bull terrier relieving itself against one of the flat front tyres.

'Er ... O...K, boss.'

Just a week later, Lucy took several small packages up to London: each package contained a written account composed from letters and phrases cut out of newspapers and a USB stick containing all the edited video evidence they had acquired. Wearing gloves she took them out of a plastic bag and posted them at Waterloo Station. Any doubts the cousins might have had about the evidence being believed were dispelled within 24 hours. All three newspapers they had sent the material to had articles about 'ongoing investigations' into alleged serious irregularities in professional conduct by a leading sporting personality and a primary school teacher. By the following day the news of Podpilasky's sudden disappearance was headline news in all the media. As one leading TV commentator said:

'A spokesperson for Mr Podpilasky says he has taken a few days off for a quiet holiday with his family but there is mounting speculation that he has in fact fled the country to a secret destination in Eastern Europe to escape possible arrest and interrogation concerning serious criminal activities.'

Following an urgent meeting of St Luigi's Board of Governors, Mr Z was suspended until further notice pending the completion of enquiries by the school, the local education authority and the police. To add to his woes, his car had disappeared overnight and was even now in Ron Pollard's garage being resprayed and fitted with new number plates.

Two kindly police officers, came to the school and spoke to all the pupils in the hall after assembly.

'One of your teachers,' an officer said, 'is currently helping us with our enquiries to do with the school football matches. If any of you feel you have anything to tell us about Mr Z which might help us – especially if he has threatened you or attempted to bribe you – you may do so in complete confidence by speaking to me or Constable Noholmes. The school office will arrange an appointment for you to see one of us during the school day.'

In the event, nobody had any complaints to make about Mr Z and although, following the various inquiries into his behaviour, he was sacked from the school, the police decided that there were not sufficient grounds on which to prosecute him. This decision was principally based upon the fact that no children had sought to incriminate him.

16

Exciting Plans

When the excitement relating to Podpilasky's disappearance and Mr Z's dismissal had started to die down, the cousins met up once again at Lucy's request.

'Grace and I have had an idea,' said Lucy. 'When I say an idea I mean a really *crazy* idea.' The others were immediately curious.

'Go on then,' said Ben impatiently.

'In the Gazette it says that there's a hotel on the edge of Wimbledon Common that's up for sale. The building is very old and beautiful but it's too expensive to renovate So the owners are selling up and retiring. What's interesting is that the hotel is in the middle of a massive park with lawns and gardens and lots of woodland – 14 hectares altogether.'

'What's a hectare?' asked Christopher.

'I looked it up. It's 10,000 square metres so this place is the size of about twenty football pitches!'

'Where are we going with all this?' asked Ben.

'Well, that place could solve both our problems. We could use one of the great big lawns as a football pitch for the Elven Rovers. We could renovate the house and use it as the football club house and then the rest of it we would keep as woods – private woods with a big fence all round where nobody could go with a mobile. Then the goblins could create a new gobblehide in there and be safe and undisturbed.' The others stared at her in disbelief, momentarily silenced by the audacious proposal.

'But that would cost a fortune!' said Ben eventually.

'We've *got* a fortune,' said Lucy calmly. 'At least the goblins have, and they're the ones who are mostly going to benefit. Alfie says they have a gigantic hoard of gold, accumulated over thousands of years. It must be worth an unbelievable amount of money. I looked up some stuff on the internet this morning. Gold is incredibly heavy. One *gram* of gold is worth twenty-five pounds. One gram. So that means each kilogram the goblins have is worth twenty-five thousand pounds! I've no idea how much they've got but I bet it's loads. Roman gold coins weighed four or five grams; a British gold sovereign weighs almost eight grams and some gold coins weigh over thirty grams. Just one cubic centimetre of gold weighs nearly twenty grams. A school lunch box packed full of gold would be worth over a million pounds. And the goblins don't just have pure gold. Most of their stuff must be fashioned into artefacts – rings, brooches, coins, bracelets, sword hilts. These are worth more than just their weight in gold because of their rarity and historical value. The goblins must have a *humungous* fortune in their gobblehide.'

'...they have a gigantic hoard of gold, accumulated over thousands of years...'

Everybody was silent as they thought about what they had just heard. It was so obviously true. The goblins could buy up that old hotel and its land a thousand times over if they wished.

'How do we persuade the goblins to give up their gold?' asked Henry.

'We get Alfie to talk to them. Once they realise that this is their only option for survival they'll have to agree.'

They discussed the project and agreed they would have to employ caretakers for the house – ideally a retired couple who would look after the house and club facilities and have free accommodation on the somewhat unusual condition that they never used a mobile phone.

'Assuming we get the gold,' said Grace, 'how do we actually go about transporting it and selling it and buying the hotel. It sounds awfully complicated.'

'It will be,' said Lucy. 'But I'm sure it can be done. In the meantime, let's talk to the goblins – otherwise it's a non-starter.'

'What if somebody else buys the hotel in the meantime?' asked Sarah.

'Good point,' said Lucy. 'But in the article it said it won't actually go on sale for another two months so we've got a bit of time to get organised. Let's go out and talk to Alfie.'

As they went Henry reported that Wayne, Darren and Dominic were all very keen on the idea of starting a football club which made them feel even more determined to press on with their plans.

A little while later they all sat round Alfie who was on an upturned flowerpot, back in his usual club strip. They had told him the whole story and were eagerly awaiting his reaction.

'It would be wonderful to have the goblins happy in their own secret wood,' he said, 'but how can I talk to them without being attacked? As you know they are now getting desperate. Also, I am worried about the gold. It is said that goblins very rarely use their gold to buy anything. They are passionately attached to it.'

'I know how you can speak to them safely,' said Sarah. The others looked enquiringly as she continued. 'Three or four of us go with Alfie with our mobiles in our hands, but not switched on. Alfie takes us to the gobblehide. Any brave goblins who are out and about will retreat when they see us. When we get to the gobblehide Alfie calls to them and says we need to talk about saving them and promise we won't switch our mobiles on if they promise not to attack him.'

'Brilliant,' said Ben, and they all agreed. Alfie looked doubtful – he was clearly terrified of the malignant creatures – but he agreed to try.

At the next opportunity they went to Wimbledon Common. Jane and Marcus had come too, for a walk, but the young ones disappeared almost immediately, ostensibly to play a game of 'forty-forty-it.'

The children were soon standing round a dense clump of impenetrable gorse which Alfie assured them was the gobblehide and they watched in fascination as he nervously called through the invisible magic barrier surrounding the den. Ben, Sarah and Grace were standing in a triangle around the gorse each prominently clutching a mobile phone.

Alfie talked for what seemed to the children like an age but was in reality about five minutes. The goblins remained invisible because they were unused ever to showing themselves to the Greatfolk. Eventually he turned round despondently. The children looked at him expectantly, hoping for something positive, but knowing from his posture and expression that the news wasn't good.

'It's kind of good and bad.' He said. 'They are being very co-operative, which was a surprise – they are obviously pretty desperate about the mess they're in. The chief goblin, Barabbas, even came out and even shook hands with me – well we crossed fists actually, but it means the same thing. They would reluctantly move to the private wood if we could guarantee there would never be any mobiles used there. But there's one big problem. Barabbas said that he could probably persuade the clan to part with some gold but that no goblin in history had ever paid up before being given what he was buying. They have to be settled in the new wood and be sure that everything is OK before they will part with a single grain of gold,' he paused and frowned. 'I think this is … I can't think of the right word … but they won't be persuaded to change their mind.'

'Non-negotiable?' said Ben.

'Yes, if that means that nothing will satisfy them except what they have decided.'

'Thank you Alfie,' said Lucy. 'Please thank the goblins and tell them we will think what to do and return soon.'

Alfie did as she asked and, somewhat dejected, they left the gobblehide and went to rejoin Jane and Marcus, having agreed to meet again very soon to review the situation.

'I've got an idea,' said Sarah. It was a fine afternoon a few days later and they were sitting around on the climbing frame in their usual places. 'I've been thinking about it a lot but I expect you'll all say it's crazy.'

'Well what is it?' said Grace. 'It'll have to be good because if the goblins won't pay before they've moved and we can't buy the place before they've paid, then we're all stuck as far as I can see.'

'It's simple,' said Sarah.

'Simple, but crazy?' said Ben.

'Yes,' she carried on with a smile. 'Simple. We have to win a lottery.' They all burst out laughing. Christopher laughed so much he actually fell off the climbing frame and had to be helped back up.

'Have you any idea,' asked Lucy, 'what the odds are against winning a lottery? You are more likely to be struck by lightning – a lot more likely – than you are to have a major win on a big lottery.'

'Ah,' said Sarah with a grin, '*you* might be. But I could win a lottery – I'll tell you how in a minute.' They all looked puzzled. 'But first of all,' she continued, 'you must have heard of Fortune Soon, the new private lottery that has been advertised.' They all nodded, it had been constantly in the news and the new company had finally managed to get permission to start up and had acquired a TV slot to compete with any existing lotteries. 'Well that lottery is much smaller than the big national lotteries of various countries so the chances of winning are much better.'

'But they are still horrendously low'. said Lucy.

'True, but that's where my secret weapon comes in. I could win and so could anyone else who was smart enough and lucky enough to be able to use Alfie.'

'Alfie!' Lucy exclaimed. 'How on earth ...?' she stopped. '... of course,' she smiled. 'Of *course*!' The others still looked puzzled and she looked at Sarah enquiringly. Sarah nodded and smiled.

'It's OK – you go ahead and tell them.'

'Well, if Sarah is thinking what I'm thinking it goes like this,' Lucy continued. 'You tell Alfie the numbers you want. You buy a ticket for the live draw and take him up to the lottery studio. He hops up to the machine – invisible of course – and climbs up the tube the balls drop down. Once he's inside he finds your balls and pops them down – making sure any other balls don't. As we know, he can move like the twinkling of an eye. It should be easy-peasy for him. They all gazed at her open-mouthed as Sarah nodded in agreement.

'Fantastic!' exclaimed Ben, at last.

'Stupendous!' said Henry.

'Ultra-cool!' said Christopher.

'There's just one problem', said Grace.

'I know,' interrupted Sarah. 'Children aren't allowed to do lotteries. But I've already thought of that. We're trying to keep the grown-ups out of this so I thought we'd ask Clare – she's old enough.'

'But isn't it sort of cheating, to win the lottery with an elf?' asked Henry.

'I've been thinking about that too,' Sarah answered. 'It is sort of cheating, but we're not taking anything off anyone that they already possess – just their very small chance of winning. What I've been thinking is that only half of the lottery money goes into prizes anyway. The rest goes to good causes and taxes and stuff. What we'll be doing in our draw is increasing the amount that goes to good causes – because when we win we'll be stopping hundreds of pets from being changed into other creatures or eaten, saving the goblins from extinction and helping young footballers. We can't *tell* anyone about the pets and the goblins so this is the only way we can do it.'

'And, of course,' added Lucy, 'we can give the money back to the lottery later when we get the gold.'

'How will we do that? asked Grace. ' – sounds a bit complicated.'

'We don't have to give it to the *lottery*,' said Ben. 'We can just give it back to the country – and that is very uncomplicated.'

'How?' said Grace.

'Well, in history last week we learnt about treasure-trove. If you find something that's made of gold or is very old, like buried treasure, then you have to report it to the police, and the treasure belongs to the queen. They put it in a museum or something and sometimes the finder gets a reward. So one day when we're digging in the lawn of our hotel to put up the goal posts we "discover" – ' he did quote signs with his fingers '– a box of treasure and report it. In that way the goblins can pay everything they owe back to the state. We can work out roughly how much treasure we need to "find" to settle the debt. We might even get a reward which we could either put into the football club or keep ourselves – we'll have earned a reward after all this!'

'That's brilliant,' said Lucy, 'but I'd do it slightly differently. If we find the box on our new property they may want to come and do archaeological research which will take years and mess up our plans for both the goblins and the football. Also, the previous owners may say that it used to be their property and they should have a share. It's much better if we find the box on *common* land. So, all we do is ask the goblins when they move their gobblehide to leave an old box of treasure behind on the Common when they move their gobblehide. They can guard it with a magic spell until we're ready and then one day we take someone's dog for a walk and he chases a rabbit into a hole, starts digging and finds the box.' Everyone agreed enthusiastically with her plan. 'Well,' she continued, looking round, 'we seem to have come a long way in a short time. Great ideas from everyone.' She paused and looked concerned.

'You OK, Henry?'

'Sort of,' he said. 'I still can't get my head round winning the lottery. It can't really be right. I don't think we can talk ourselves into saying it's OK.'

'I agree,' said Lucy, 'and it's good that you're so honest. I think, if we do this, we have to accept that it's not perfectly

OK but that we're doing the best we can to sort out a problem that nobody else knows about and which we can never tell anybody about. It's like telling a white lie to avoid some greater harm or distress. I think we need to vote on it. A unanimous vote would be required before we go ahead. Would that make you feel better?'

'Yes it would. I just didn't like the idea that we were *pretending* it was all fine.' He gave a little grin and put his hand up. 'I vote to go ahead – but we've got to see what Clare and Alfie think.' And with that, they all put their hands up. And so it was decided.

17

How to Win a Lottery

It was the day they planned to win the Fortune Soon lottery. They had chosen the Saturday carefully to coincide with the last day of Clare's university term, so that she would be back home with the family shortly after the news of her win got out, and they could start putting their plans into action. As arranged, Clare had bought a ticket for the draw and texted the numbers to Lucy, who had applied weeks ahead for two tickets for herself and her friend Hannah to be in the live studio audience that evening. Everybody had agreed that it would be too suspicious for all the children suddenly to take an interest in the lottery. Joanna assumed it was really Hannah who was interested in going to the studio and Lucy said nothing to disillusion her. The rest of the cousins were going to watch on television.

Alfie was to accompany Lucy and Hannah, and Lucy prayed that there would be no hitch in their plans. Alfie could understand her but could not easily speak to her, and it was not really feasible for Christopher to come along.

As this private lottery had only been running for a month

Lucy didn't know in advance how popular the show would be so Alfie had flown to the office where the applications were sorted. As it happened the new show was booked up for weeks ahead, but Alfie saw that for every show several seats were held back in case some celebrity applied at the last moment. He simply transferred two of these reserve seats to Lucy's application form and they received their front row tickets in the post the very next day.

As soon as Lucy and Hannah had found their seats Alfie left them and flew to the lottery machine. He had glanced once at the numbers Lucy had shown him and instantly memorised them. So quickly did he look that Lucy felt she had to check that he knew them. Alfie laughed and Lucy could just make out his reply:

'Trust ... me ... I'm ... an ... elf'!'

There was a roll of drums and the compère of the show appeared. He introduced the celebrity who had been chosen to press the button to activate the machine for the draw and after the usual pleasantries asked her to proceed.

Lucy, her cousins at home and Clare packing boxes in her room in Oxford all held their breath. Could this really be happening? Could it really work?

'And now,' said the compère, 'the first number this evening is ...' he paused and looked in amazement as the ball that had started to fall down the tube seemed to reverse and rise back up into the swirling mass of balls, only to be replaced by another which successfully fell down the tube and into the gully leading it to its final position. '...well, that is *incredible*. The first ball must have had a special spin imparted to it by the swirler and has backtracked. I've never seen that before, but it all adds to the wonderful unpredictability and excitement of this event. And the first number, as you can see, is 27.' The cousins at home looked at each other then did a high-five. This was one of their numbers. There was then a long pause during which no balls entered the tube.

'Curious,' said the compère, 'quite a long delay tonight – the balls are usually fighting with each other to give someone a prize.' Suddenly a ball rose from the very bottom of the swirling mass and flicked straight into the tube. 'Ah, here we are,' said the compère, visibly relieved that the system hadn't failed. 'The second at last and it's ... 23! Let's hope,' he continued, 'that the next number finds its place a bit quicker – and so it does – *no*, it's fallen back and is replaced by ...' he paused to make quite sure that this ball knew what it was doing. As it hit the final gully he continued, '... by 9!' The cousins exchanged excited glances: all three of the numbers called so far had been correct. And so it continued. As the last ball entered the tube Lucy's fingers were white as she gripped the edge of her seat. She stared at the ball – it was the wrong number. Alfie – trying to show off how good he was at memorising – had got it wrong!

'Oh my goodness!' It was the compère. 'Believe me folks, I've never seen anything like this.' Lucy looked back to the machine. The ball had passed down almost to the bottom of the vertical tube and was about to fall into the final gully when it started to rise and return to

'Believe me folks, I've never seen anything like this...'

the general pool of balls. 'The backspin on that ball,' the compère continued, his voice trembling with excitement, 'is absolutely incredible. It has actually crept back up that tube and another ball is now descending. Will it do the same thing? No! it's moving down to its final position. And the final number is … 35!' The cousins at home whooped for joy and hugged each other; even as they did so the phone rang as Clare joined in the celebrations. But on the TV the compère had more to say:

'And now we have two special announcements to make,' he continued. 'The first is that on our VIP guest list this evening we are very fortunate to have Professor Newstein, professor of physics at Cambridge University. Our producer has consulted him and he assures us that the somewhat unusual behaviour of our balls this evening is entirely within normal statistical probability limits for balls of this size. The chances of balls spinning backwards are very small, but definitely possible. My apologies for having kept you waiting for confirmation of the final results but our engineer has just been checking the entire system. He assures me that there is no mechanical fault and no evidence that any of the equipment has been tampered with. I therefore have pleasure in confirming that this evening's results are entirely valid.' There was applause at this announcement, which the compère eventually stopped by raising both hands. 'I am pleased to announce, however, that, as a gesture of goodwill and to reassure those who might feel unhappy about tonight's results, notwithstanding the advice we have been given by our academic and engineering experts, the lottery organisers Fortune Soon have just sent me a message.' He read from a note handed to him by a steward. 'Any lottery ticket used in tonight's draw will also be valid for the next mid-week draw – with the exception, of course ...' he smiled smugly, '... of this evening's winners.'

At this there was tumultuous applause and Lucy knew that Henry would at last feel comfortable about the evening's events. And so it was that Clare won the lottery and came home as planned the following day. Within a few days an extremely large sum of tax-free money was credited to her bank account. Minutes later the phone rang.

'Can I speak to Miss Clare Bonaventure please.'

'Speaking,' said Clare.

'Oh, hello, this is Sharon at the Hoarders Bank, how are you doing today?'

'At last,' said Clare, ignoring the pointless and insincere question. 'I've been ringing you for two weeks but can never get to speak to a real person. I've made about ten phone calls and the system says you'll ring me back but nobody ever does – at least not until now. Anyway, you said I was overdrawn £2.50 on my account – which I wasn't – and you've charged me a massive penalty fee. So please can you refund my money and make sure the system knows I have never been overdrawn so it doesn't affect my credit rating.' There was an embarrassed pause.

'Er, I wasn't ringing about that, Miss Bonaventure. I was ringing about the money that's just been credited to your account. The bank wants to advise ...'

'So!' Clare interrupted, 'when I want you to correct a mistake, I can't get through to you for two weeks, but when I've got some money that you want a slice of you ring me within seconds of its being deposited in my account. Well I don't want any of your advice, thank you, and if anyone else pesters me about this I'm going to change banks. Oh – and refund that penalty fee. *Now*! Goodbye.' She put the phone down and turned to Lucy. 'There! I feel much better now.'

But, having said this, she suddenly felt overcome with the enormity of what she had done and the reality of having a fortune in her bank account. As soon as she could arrange it she called all the cousins together and told them it was time to get the adults involved. They were all beginning to feel the same way, though hadn't liked to be the first to say so, so that evening both sets of cousins told their parents the whole story. Clare also told their grandparents as she thought they would have more time than anyone else in the family to start buying the property if they were happy to do so. The adults were amazed to hear what the younger ones had been up to and Jane was relieved to learn at last what all those secret meetings had been about. With the families' experience of Lucy the news of Christopher's power was not treated with the disbelief and astonishment that it would have been in any other family.

As Richard said later:

'If we had known about this plan beforehand we would never have agreed, but as we've been presented with a *fait accompli* we may as well help to make it work as best we can.'

And the focus was soon on sorting out the practical details of acquiring the property that was needed to solve the goblins' problems.

Grandpa and Grandma agreed to act as Clare's agents in dealing with the estate agents and lawyers and within a few weeks the deal was done and the goblins safely installed. The disappearance of the pets came to an abrupt end, and as far as the public was concerned, became a mystery that was never solved. Several books were written about the case and a film was eventually made which – to the great amusement of the cousins who knew what had actually happened – was about a restaurant that made kebabs out of the stolen pets and was closed down for quite other health and safety issues, thereby bringing an end to the 'petnapping saga' as it was called.

It was a warm summer's evening and the Bonaventures and the Sharps were relaxing on the terrace of the beautiful old hotel they had bought. Richard and Marcus were lighting the barbecue, Jane and Joanna were sitting on a swinging garden chair discussing the renovations to the hotel which were due to start the following Monday, the youngsters were eating crisps and drinking lemonade, and Grandpa was opening a bottle of champagne and chatting animatedly with Michael who had just returned from his search for yetis in the Himalayas.

The goblins had been warned about the building work at the house. To protect them from the builders' mobiles Grandpa had created a very large cordon around the property similar to a police incident area, about 50 yards away from the house, with a bright yellow tape attached to trees and posts. Alfie had asked the goblins how close they could safely come to a mobile, and Grandpa had added an extra margin just to be sure.

While they were eating, Henry suddenly asked Jane what had happened to Mr Z. Jane was a parent governor at St Luigi's and usually knew the school gossip.

'Well, he's been sacked as you know,' she answered, 'and he's most unlikely to get a job at another school. I heard he was giving some private sporting tuition but it's going to be very hard for him to make a living. Oh – and apparently he's given up smoking.'

'What!' said Ben. 'The whole school knows he smokes a million fags a day. Why on earth should he give up – especially after what's happened to him?'

'I think I know why,' said Henry. He paused, looking a little uncomfortable.

'Well go on,' said Ben. 'Why?'

'Well ... ' he hesitated again, as the others had fallen silent and were now listening. '... well on one of the videos Alfie took to check on what Lackey was telling Z- man to do there was a clip of Z-man talking to Miss Summer – she's my form teacher,' he added for the girls' benefit. 'I felt a bit guilty seeing it which is why I never mentioned it before, but I think he must have asked her out. In the clip she was telling him she was sorry but she could never go out with a smoker. So, now I think that she may be the reason he's given up.'

'Well that's really juicy gossip,'said Jane, 'but your first instincts were right and it's none of our business so we'll all forget all about it. Now before we got onto his smoking, Henry, why were you asking about Mr Z ?'

'I ... ' he paused again, uncertain as to how the others would react. '... I was just thinking. He wasn't really *bad*, he was just greedy and now I feel a bit – a bit sorry for him. And,' he added hurriedly before anyone could disagree with him, 'he is a fantastic PE teacher.'

'So what?' asked Ben.

'Well, I was just wondering ... we've got the money from the lottery to help the goblins and get our football club launched, and Mum's going to interview people to look after the house, but we haven't actually got anyone to run the club.'

'What!' exclaimed Ben. 'You're not actually suggesting that we employ that crook as our club manager are you?' Henry looked embarrassed.

'Well – yes, I suppose I am or at least as the coach to start with. He must have had a massive fright over what's happened and I can't believe he'll start trying to be dishonest again. And Grandma says she'll look after the club accounts so she wouldn't let him diddle her by one penny.'

There was a long silence while everybody digested what had just been said.

'Well I think it's a brilliant idea,' said Lucy eventually. 'People will soon forget about his being sacked and he sounds like such a good football teacher that he'll soon establish a reputation for the club.'

'And,' added Jane, 'it would be generous and charitable to give him a fresh start and help him restore his reputation.'

'But there won't be enough for him to do, will there?' said Sarah.

'Not at first,' said Jane. 'We could appoint him as combined coach and manager and he'd have to start part-time, but he could probably carry on with his private coaching. At least though he'd have a proper basic job and as the club grows he could gradually do more and more.'

They discussed it at length and eventually agreed unanimously that they would invite him to be the club coach and manager.

The proposal was that training would start immediately and continue over the summer holidays, and the first match could be at the start of the next season in early autumn.

18

A Fresh Start

It was the beginning of September and the sun was shining in a cloudless sky.

The newly refurbished and freshly painted hotel sparkled in the morning light. The caretakers, a retired restaurant manager and his wife, bustled about preparing coffees and teas and a long table was covered in pies, sausage rolls, sandwiches, cakes and biscuits.

Richard and Jane stood on the terrace listening to the excited buzz of conversation and looking out at the shining new goals and pristine white markings of the football pitch that had been created on the great lawn in front of them. They still found it hard to believe this was really happening. Christopher, the youngest of their children, after a minor accident could actually speak to elves and as a result of that they were all here. In a few moments the Elven Rovers would christen the new club pitch with their first matches – a boys' friendly against Worcester Park followed by a girls' friendly against a Kingston team in which Sarah would be captaining the Elven Rovers against her old club.

After these matches Christopher and some friends from his class would be playing against the other class in their school year.

There was a notice politely requesting spectators not to use their mobile phones "in order to preserve a relaxed and carefree atmosphere." There was a brand new interwoven panelled wood fence, 2 metres high, separating the pitch from the rest of the grounds, and this fence continued around the entire area the two families now referred to among themselves as the goblin reservation. The goblins had already been warned about the matches but as an additional precaution to protect them there was a warning system. Whenever the football car park gate was open an electronic switch automatically turned on a warning light outside the gobblehide so that any forgetful goblin emerging from the den would know to keep well away from the football fence that day.

And now, at last, the moment had come. The Bonaventure and Sharp families stood expectantly on the touchline.

Henry stood in the centre of the field with Darren and Wayne on either side. Joshua was in midfield, Dominic and Adam were backs and Max was in goal.

There were no elves on the field, but many were invisibly clustered on the goal cross-bars. Richard and Marcus were linesmen.

Z-man walked importantly on to the field and took up his position. He looked relaxed and content. He glanced over to the touchline where Miss Summer was standing next to Jane. She gave him a little wave of encouragement and as she did so the sun flashed and sparkled on the stones in her new ring. Oskar looked looked at his watch and started to put his whistle to his lips. It was time to start the game and a new life. He paused for a moment, looked across, and winked at the three strikers. Henry looked at Wayne.

'It's been quite a year hasn't it?' he said. Wayne grinned.

'I'm not big on history. Just make sure you pass to me and not my idiot brother.'

Henry grinned back. The whistle blew. Darren took Henry's pass cleanly, moved forward and the game was on. Out of trial and tribulation – and magic – a new club was born and it was destined for great things.

Epilogue

THE WIMBLEDON GAZETTE
(Thursday 8th September)
Largest-ever Treasure-Trove
by R Stiltskin, our financial affairs correspondent

A group of children playing hide-and-seek on Wimbledon Common last Saturday have uncovered the largest hoard of gold and silver ever discovered in Britain. The trove of 6000 pieces includes gold and silver coins, and a breathtaking collection of exquisitely crafted jewellery, ornaments, swords and armour. The find, which dwarfs previous large collections such as the Sutton Hoo Trove (1939) and the Staffordshire Hoard (2009) is unique among such discoveries in that its contents are not confined, as are most such collections, to a particular historical period. Experts are completely baffled by the fact that this hoard contains pre-civilization precious metals and stones, and artefacts from the dawn of civilization up to the modern day. Unworked gold nuggets and primitive pots full of grains of gold sit next to coins and jewellery from Phoenicia, Troy, Egypt, Lydia, Ancient Greece and Rome. There are large collections of Bronze Age, Anglo-Saxon and medieval treasures, and hoards of precious items from every subsequent century up to the modern day.

Historians are fascinated by the inclusion in the hoard of items of such varied provenance as Inca gold (presumably plundered by English pirates from the Spanish Main), coins from the Napoleonic wars, Krugerrands, treasure believed to have been plundered in Nazi Europe and, perhaps the most astonishing of all, bullion thought to emanate from the Brink's-Mat robbery from a Heathrow warehouse in 1983. Most of this stolen gold was never recovered and quite how it has come to be part of this treasure hoard will probably forever remain a mystery. Archaeologists, historians, art experts and museum directors are flooding into Wimbledon from all over the world.

'It's worse than tennis fortnight,' said one local resident, unable to get to work because of the traffic.

'How much is all this worth?' I asked one expert from the British Museum.

'Quite impossible to say,' came the reply. 'Some of the artwork is simply beyond price. But to try and answer your question, we are talking hundreds of millions or possibly even billions.'

The children who made this stupendous discovery wish to remain anonymous for obvious reasons and we will respect their request for privacy. The hoard is classed *as treasure-trove and is automatically the property of the Crown. A discretionary reward, however, is often given to the finders of such treasure and we have learnt that if such a reward is given in this case the children wish for it to be donated to the good causes espoused by the new Fortune Soon lottery.*

What wonderful young people! God bless you, whoever you are; you have restored the faith of many across the land in the younger generation!

The End

Appendix

(See chapter four. Christopher has just asked the elf what the word elvensib means)

'Well it's one of my closest relations,' replied the elf. We don't have brothers or sisters like you humans – just elvensibs.'

'But ...' Christopher didn't quite know how to ask the question. '... but, if there aren't any brothers and sisters then where do men and women elves come from?' The elf smiled.

'They don't come from anywhere because they don't exist. Elves are all just like me and we're all the same – a bit like angels I suppose: no boys and no girls. On the rare occasions that we appear to Greatfolk they see us as they imagine us to be. You see me as a boy-elf but a girl might see me as a girl-elf.'

'So ... you haven't got a mother or father ?'
'Correct.'
'Well where did you come from?'
There is a special cave in the far west of this land – in your tongue it is called Cornwall – that is very old.

Unbelievably old. I'm told there are similar caves in other lands. In that cave there is a special pool. Every thousand years in your time a great big blob of something, invisible to you and all animals, turns into something like frog spawn with millions of tiny eggs in it. Within a few days each little egg hatches into an elf and as soon as their wings are dry they fly off all over the land. They seem by instinct to go to the places where elves have always lived and if they get lost the fairies tell them where to go. The fairies seem to be immortal.'

'Wow,' breathed Christopher. He'd always found the notion of immortality to be a mind-blowing concept but to be faced with it in the actual existence of fairies on earth was almost impossible to contemplate. He pushed the thought to the back of his mind and concentrated on the elves.

'But what happens after a thousand years?'

'We all return to the cave. It must seem a long time to you who have such short lives, but I think time seems to pass differently for the Greatfolk and Littlefolk.

We gather together in the same place that we were born and somehow magically dissolve into that mysterious blob from which we started. That then remains dormant – asleep – for a year and a day and then spawning starts again. Among all the Littlefolk it is called the Elvenbirth. So we never really die – we sort of reform and rejuvenate.'

'Like a Phoenix – but with water instead of fire!' said Christopher, who had just learnt about the mythical bird at school.

'Exactly,' agreed the elf. 'In fact it's curious that you should mention that amazing creature for there is actually a phoenipyre on a crag above our own magic cave.'

'Phoenipyre?' asked Christopher.

'That's the special place where they come to be reborn. It is surrounded by a magic barrier through which none can pass.'

'That's amazing!' said Christopher. 'I can't wait to tell them all at scho ...' he stopped. He couldn't tell anybody at school. In fact, maybe he couldn't tell *anybody*. People would all laugh and think he was completely barmy. Again the worry flooded over him that maybe he *was*. But the elf seemed so real... He wrenched his mind back to the present and forced himself to return to their conversation.

'How old are you now? I mean – if that's not a rude thing to ask?'

'I'm just over 136.'

'Gosh!' was all Christopher could say. What, he wondered, must this little being have seen in his – its – life? 'So in another ...' he paused to do the arithmetic '... in another eight hundred and sixty-four years you go back to have a new Elvenbirth – right? The elf nodded. 'And then you kind of ... hibernate ... for a year and a day, then come back to life?' Another nod. 'But how do you know it's a year and a day if you're asleep? In fact, how do you know about any of this?'

'You're a smart kid,' said the elf, 'for it's a very good question. But the answer is disappointingly simple – we know because the fairies have told us. As I told you they seem to just go on and on and they are so powerful they control all the world of magical creatures like me, the Littlefolk: hobgoblins, goblins, pixies, sprites, leprechauns, brownies, imps, nymphs, hobs and many others – some incredibly rare. When I say the fairies "control" all these creatures I must explain this in more detail. The fairies are more powerful than all of us and their magic is unassailable. But they have a strict code – The Faerie Code or Ancient Code – which has existed since time began and this governs their behaviour. It lays down when, for instance they can interfere or intervene in human affairs, when they can interfere with animals and insects – over which they can exert complete control if they wish – and when and how they intervene in the affairs of the Littlefolk.'

'What's your name?' asked Christopher, 'Or don't you have names?'

'Oh, we do but, because we don't have any parents, we choose our names ourselves when we are fully grown – that's when we are about one day old. We then keep that name for a thousand years and choose a new one after our 'hibernation.' I actually chose my present name in my previous Elvenbirth but I liked it and chose it again this time so I've had it for over eleven hundred years.'

'And what is it?'

'I'm called Aelfred because that Elvenbirth occurred during the reign of one king of the Greatfolk who that name. In fact his name means 'elf counsel.' He loved the Littlefolk and made his servants put out food and drink for us every day. This amused us because we would have stolen it anyway – it's one of the mischievous things we do – but it made us realize he was a kind and good king .'

(Now return to chapter four).

Animal and Elven Lexicon

(Author's note: Some of these names start with upper-case [capital] letters and some with lower-case. The upper-case indicates names that are held in particular regard by animals, magical beings or human beings. The suffix -kin can be either singular or plural)

Ancient Code	see Faerie Code
animanet	animal communication network
Bennikin	Ben Sharp
Brilliant One	the sun
Christiekin	Christopher Sharp
coneyhop	a rabbit
dreykin	a squirrel
elfnook	an elfin home
elvenbirth	the rejuvenation process for elves
Elvenfolk	the elfin species
elvensib	an elf born in the same elvenbirth as another elf
Faerie Code	the ancient rules governing the behaviour of all magical beings

Feathered folk	all bird species
furriclaws	a cat
Furrykin	all mammalian species
gobblehide	a goblin home
grandkin	a grandchild
Great Salt	the sea
Great Silver One	the moon
Greatfolk	humankind
greatkin	grandparent
hedgiquill	a hedgehog
Hiddenkin	the animals' name for all magical beings
hobblehide	a hobgoblin home
Littlefolk	all magical beings
manefang	a lion
nightbane	an owl
phoenipyre	the pyre (*qv*) on which a phoenix cremates itself
Promised One	Lucy Bonaventure
scurripod	a rat, mouse, vole, etc.
stripedfang	a tiger
sunsleep	night-time
Tailless One	a human being
Wraithkin	another name for the Hiddenkin (see above and see Glossary)

Notes on the Names in the Book

These notes give some information about the people and places referred to in the book, and cite the chapter or section in which their name first appears. Some of the names are real and the information given is simply factual. Many of the names, however, are fictitious, or used in a fictitious manner, and these tell you something about the character to whom they belong. Unusual words or abbreviations used in this section are explained in the glossary.

Aelfred (*Chapter 4 and appendix*) Alfred the Great (849– 899) was the king of Wessex – an Anglo-Saxon kingdom in southern England. For almost thirty years Alfred fought to protect England from the Viking invaders. He was a wise and just man. The name Aelfred means "elf counsel" or "wise elf."

Al Burno (*Chapter 1*) This is Ben's favourite restaurant but it sounds as if the food might be overcooked!

Ariel (*Chapter 8*) Ariel, like the elf named after him in this book, is a magical spirit of the air. He appears in William Shakespeare's famous play *The Tempest*.

Barabbas (*Chapter 16*) Barabbas, the chief goblin, shares a name with the notorious prisoner released instead of Jesus by the Roman governor Pontius Pilate at the insistence of the crowd in the New Testament.

Blenheim spot (*Chapter 13*) The dog belonging to Liz Canamans is a Cavalier King Charles spaniel. Some of these dogs have a characteristic brown spot in the middle of the forehead. Legend has it that Sarah Churchill, the Duchess of Malborough, pressed her thumb hard on the head of her pregnant female spaniel while anxiously awaiting news about her husband fighting in the Battle of Blenheim. The battle was won and when the spaniel had five puppies they all bore the lucky thumb mark on their forehead. This survives to this day in their descendants!

Bonaventure (*Prologue et seq.*) Bonaventure is the surname of the boys' cousins. St Bonaventure (1221–74) was a mystic and philosopher who was the author of *The Life of Saint Francis*. St Francis, like Lucy and Grace, was said to be able to communicate with animals.

Canamans (*Chapter 13*) Canamans is combination of the Latin words *canis* meaning dog and *amans* meaning lover. A good name for a dog owner!

Cat and Fox (*Chapter 13*) The name of an imaginary public house in Wimbedon.

Chessington World of Adventures Resort (*Chapter 10 et seq.*) A theme park and zoo situated southwest of London.

Chubby (*Chapter 6*) Mr Yale the caretaker is called 'Chubby' by the boys because he is plump. This nickname is also similar to that of a type of lock and Chubby locks up the school. Also see Yale.

Dr Pixel (*Chapter 3*) Dr Andy Pixel is the radiologist who looks at Christopher's X-ray and scan images on a display screen. A *pixel* is one of the tiny dots that make up the picture on a screen.

Dragon's Fury (*Chapter 10*) A roller coaster ride at Chessington World of Adventures Resort.

Duffer's Preparatory School (*Chapter 7*) A duffer is a person who is unskilful, incompetent or slow to learn. It seems likely that this is not a very good school football team.

Forty-forty-it (*Chapter 16*) A hide-and-seek game in which one person (the seeker) stands by a central feature (eg a rock or a tree) and counts up to a predetermined number while all the other participants go off and hide. The seeker then tries to find those hiding. Those who can sneak back to the central feature without being touched by the seeker are safe The first person touched by the seeker becomes the next seeker. (Also called 'block' and other local names).

Furrowhead (*Chapter 3*) Professor Furrowhead is a brain surgeon who makes *furrows* in *heads*.

Gormless (*Chapter 1 et seq.*) The Gormless twins live up to their name (see gormless in the glossary).

Himalayas (*Prologue*) A mountain range stretching across northeastern India. The range passes through India, Pakistan, Afghanistan, Nepal, Bhutan, Tibet and China. It includes some of the highest mountains in the world.

Hoarders Bank (*Chapter 17*) A hoard is a store of something valuable or useful hidden away for future use. A bank is just what a hoarder needs!

Hope Preparatory School (*Chapter 2*) This school is *hoping* to win the football league.

Ingots Preparatory School (*Chapter 1 et seq.*) This rich private school is well-named, for an ingot is a bar of gold.

Jupiter (*Chapter 1 et seq.*) Mr Jupiter is the head teacher at St Luigi's. It is an appropriate name for a school head, for Jupiter (Zeus) was the King of the Gods in Ancient Roman and Greek mythology!

Just William (*Chapter 7*) William Brown is a mischievous boy who is the hero of many famous children's stories written by Richmal Crompton.

Lackey (*Chapter 3 et seq.*) Alan Lackey is Mr. Podpilasky's loyal assistant. He has a suitable name for the word 'lackey' means a servile follower.

Len Hutton (*Chapter 3 et seq.*) A good name for a PE teacher. Sir Leonard 'Len' Hutton (1916–1990) was captain of the England cricket team and is regarded as one of the greatest batsmen in the history of the game.

Newstein (*Chapter 17*) The distinguished professor of physics in this story has a name which contains elements of the names of two of the world's most famous scientists. Who are they?

Noholmes (*Chapter 15*) Police Constable Noholmes also appeared in the first book in this series: *The Promised*

One. He is still a constable after several years and we think he is not a very good detective. Certainly not as good as *Sherlock Holmes*, the famous fictional detective in the books written by Sir Arthur Conan Doyle.

Obama (*Chapter 1*) Obama is originally an African name meaning 'bent', a very appropriate name for the crooked character in this story!

Outlaws (*Chapter 7*) 'The Outlaws' is the name of William Brown's gang (see *Just William* above). An outlaw is a criminal on the run from the police.

Pethasgone (*Chapter 13*) Gloria is well-named because her pet-has-gone!

Petula Paucity (*Chapter 13*) Petula is reporting on the mysterious *paucity* of *pets* (see glossary).

Podpilasky (*Chapter 1 et seq.*) The Greek root *pod* (from *podos*) means foot; *pilos* was a Greek ballgame and – *asky* is an eastern European name ending. So Podpilasky is a footballer from eastern Europe!

Pollard (*Chapter 2 et seq.*) Ron Pollard is, of course, the brother of the wicked lumberjack Pollard who tries to kill Lucy in *The Promised One*. His account of the incident involving his brother is somewhat different to Lucy's!

Rameses Revenge (*Chapter 11*) A famous adventure ride at Chessington World of Adventures Resort.

R Stiltskin (*Epilogue*) This journalist is the financial affairs correspondent of the Wimbledon Gazette. *Rumpelstiltskin* features in an ancient German fairytale that is included in a collection of stories published by the Brothers Grimm in 1812. He is an imp who can spin straw into gold so this is a very appropriate name for a journalist who writes about money.

St. Jude's (*Chapter 7*) St. Jude's is the name of the school that is so bad at football that St. Luigi's were confident of beating them easily. St. Jude, however, is the patron saint of lost causes and he certainly lives up to his name in Chapter seven!

St Luigi's (*Prologue et seq.*) This is where Henry and Christopher go to school. It is a good name for a school so interested in football, for St Luigi Scrosoppi (1804–1884) is the patron saint of football. His feast day is celebrated on 5th October.

St Mediocre's (*Chapter 6*) St Mediocre's is one of the schools playing against St Luigi's in the football league. Their name suggests they are not very good (see *mediocre* in the glossary).

St. Sapientia's (*Chapter 10*) St. Sapientia's is the school attended by Lucy, Grace and Sarah. *Sapientia* is the Latin word for wisdom.

Stanley Matthews (*Chapter 3 et seq.*) A good name for a PE teacher. Sir Stanley Matthews (1915–2000), nicknamed 'Wizard of the Dribble', was still playing top-league football at the age of fifty! He is regarded as one of the greatest English footballers of all time.

Yale (*Chapter 6*) Mr. Yale, the school caretaker who locks up at night, is well-named. *Linus Yale* invented a famous type of lock in about 1850 which is still used throughout the world.

Yeti (*Prologue*) A Hominoid cryptid reported principally from the Himalayan mountains. The name derives from Tibetan roots meaning 'rock bear' and the creature has many other appellations, including '*The Abominable Snowman*', '*Meh-teh*' (man bear) and '*Mizo*' (wild man). Himalayan folklore is steeped with traditions about a man-like creature leaving footprints in the snow and occasionally glimpsed among the trees or snow-covered rocks in remote mountain sites. Some cryptozoologists believe it may be an extant example of the ape gigantopithecus, the largest ape that ever lived, but this is thought by mainstream science to have been long extinct (100 thousand years ago). Sceptics think that the yeti sightings may actually be those of the langur monkey, the Tibetan blue bear, or the Himalayan brown or red bear. A theory that the animal is a subspecies of polar bear seems to have been discounted by recent DNA studies on hair samples.

Zdradzacski (*Chapter 1 et.seq.*) Oskar is well-named. Zdradzać is an eastern European word meaning to be false or to cheat!

Glossary

The explanations in this glossary give only the meanings of words as they are used in the book. Many of the words have other meanings as well, and if a full description of a word is required the interested reader should consult a dictionary. If a word in the explanation is followed by (qv) then please look up that word in the glossary for further information.

(*abbrev.* — abbreviation, *adj.* — adjective, *adv.* — adverb, *conj.* — conjunction, *n.* — noun, *pl.n.* — plural noun, *prep.* — preposition, *v.* — verb, *intrans.v* — intransitive verb)

absorb *v.* to take in; to receive; to suck up

abysmal *adj.* very bad; terrible

accusation *n.* an allegation that someone is guilty of a crime, misdemeanour or offence; an imputation or charge

acquire *v.* to get something; to obtain; to gain possession

acronym *n.* a pronounceable word made up from some or all of the initial letters of a longer title eg: NATO – The North Atlantic Treaty Organization

adorn *v.* to make beautiful; to decorate

advisor *n.* one who gives advice or guidance

aeon *n.* an unimaginably long period of time

aerial *adj.* to do with the air or aircraft; in or of the air

affluence *n.* abundant wealth; the possession of riches

afoot *adj.* in operation; happening at that time

aggro *n.* (slang) an abbreviation of *aggravation* meaning annoyance or nuisance

ajar *adj.* slightly open

akin *adj.* similar; having the same characteristics

albeit *conj.* even though; notwithstanding

alpha male *n.* the dominant male in a group of animals or people

analysis *n.* the process of examining something to determine its composition, or the results obtained by doing so

animated *adj.* lively; full of vivacity

annexe *n.* something added, especially a supplement to a document

anonymous *adj.* from or by an unknown person

apparition *n.* something that appears, such as a ghost or spectre

apprehension *n.* a state of fear or anxiety about something that might happen

archaeology *n.* the study of human history by the examination of buildings, materials and artefacts left from previous cultures

arrogant *adj.* conceited; boastful; proud

artefact *n.* a man-made article

ashen *adj.* pale; pallid; drained of colour; like ashes

audacious *adj.* daring; bold

avian *adj.* relating to or resembling a bird

babble *n.* chatter; incoherent or meaningless speech

barmy *adj.* (slang) mad; insane

beacon *n.* a signal; a light or fire to attract attention

bewilder *v.* to confuse; to perplex; to puzzle

biceps *n.* a two-headed flexor muscle in the upper arm

bidding *n.* order; command; summons

bizarre *adj.* very odd; unusual – especially in an amusing or interesting way

blackmail *n.* the use of threats (usually of revealing a secret) to get money or, as in Chapter 1, to influence the actions of another

Blenheim spot *n.* see above in *Notes on the names in the book*

bonobo *n.* a species of pygmy chimpanzee (*Pan Paniscus*) found in the Congo

bonus *n.* a payment or gift that is greater than the expected reward

booming *adj.* (*slang*) performing very well; highly successful

bribe *n.* a gift of money or goods in exchange for a favour

brownie *n.* (*folklore*) a type of elf supposed to do helpful chores at night, especially housework

bulky *adj.* very large

burly *adj.* thickset in build; large and sturdy

butt *n.* a cigarette stub

cajole *v.* to coax; to wheedle; to persuade, especially by flattery

castigate *v.* to rebuke; to criticize severely

CCTV *abbrev.* closed-circuit television

cf. *abbrev. confer (Latin)* compare; see. Used to guide the reader to another source of information

chain-smoke *v.* to smoke one cigarette after another – often lighting a new cigarette from the previous one

chandelier *n.* a hanging light with several ornamental branches for candles or bulbs

chauffeur *n.* one employed to drive a car

chisel *n.* a sharp blade used to carve wood or stone: hence 'chiselled' meaning finely crafted or cleanly cut

chubby *adj.* plump; fat; round

clammy *adj.* unpleasantly moist or sticky

clan *n.* a group of people who are related; a tribe

clunk *n.* a metallic thud

cluster *v.* to gather round in a close group

colloquial *adj.* informal; conversational; idiomatic

collude *v.* to plot together; to connive; to conspire

commercial *adj.* to do with buying and selling; connected with business

comparison *n.* judging or comparing one thing against another

compère *n.* the person running a show; the master of ceremonies

compliance *n.* the act of agreeing; going along with a plan

comprehension *n.* understanding

conceal *v.* to hide something or someone; to keep secret

concept *n.* an idea; a theory

concussion *n.* loss of consciousness following a blow on the head

confer *v.* to bestow upon; to endow; to grant

confidential *adj.* secret; private

console *v.* to comfort; to bring solace

conspiracy *n.* a secret plot to carry out a harmful act

conspirator *n.* one who plots in secret with another or others

contemplate *v.* to think about intently; to consider

contingency *n.* something that could or might happen; an eventuality

conviction *n.* being found guilty of an offence or crime

cordial *adj.* friendly; warm; agreeable

cordon *n.* a chain, rope (etc.) or line of people stationed around an area to protect or isolate it

courteous *adj.* polite; considerate

crag *n.* a peak; a rugged point on a rock

cremate *v.* to burn to ashes – especially a corpse

Cretaceous period *n.* the last period of the Mesozoic era, between the Jurassic and Tertiary periods, 144-65 million years ago

crock *n.* an earthenware pot

crucial *adj.* essential; critically important

cryptid *n.* a cryptozoological term for a creature rumoured to exist but not recognized by mainstream science

cutlery *n.* tableware such as knives, forks and spoons

damning *adj.* providing proof of guilt

deflect *v.* to turn something aside from its course; to cause something to swerve

defraud *v.* to swindle; to steal by cheating

dejected *adj.* downcast; despondent; miserable

delirious *adj.* wildly excited with joy

deluge *n.* an overwhelming number (literally: a flood)

demonstration *n.* a display to show how something works

demoralize *v.* to dishearten; to undermine

despondent *adj.* dejected; downcast; hopeless; disheartened

destined *adj.* decided in advance; pre-ordained

detach *v.* to split off; to separate; to remove

deteriorate *v.* to get worse

diddle *v.* (slang) to swindle; to cheat

digit *n.* a finger or toe

diminish *v.* to reduce; to make smaller

diminutive *adj.* very small; tiny

disable *v.* to put out of action; to make ineffective

discomfiture *n.* the state of being uneasy or uncomfortable

disdainful *adj.* showing scorn or contempt; acting in a superior manner

dishearten *v.* to destroy or weaken one's courage, hope, enthusiasm etc.

disillusion *v.* to change someone's falsely hopeful ideas; to reveal the truth to another

dismissal *n.* being removed or sacked from a post or job

dispel *v.* to drive away; to disperse

disperse *v.* to break up; to scatter

disruptive *adj.* causing turmoil or disorder

distraction *n.* something that diverts the attention

distraught *adj.* very upset; agitated; distracted

ditch *v.* (*slang*) to discard; to get rid of; to abandon

DIY *abbrev.* Do It Yourself. Doing jobs around the house yourself instead of using a professional

dock *n.* a common broad-leaved plant. The leaf is commonly used to soothe the pain caused by a stinging nettle

dominate *v.* to be the most important; to tower above all else

dork *n.* (*slang*) a stupid or incompetent person

dormant *adj.* in a resting or inactive state; sleepy or asleep

downright *adj.* used to make another word stronger. In Chapter 6 it means Z-man is *really* scared

draft *v.* to prepare; to compose

dryad *n.* (*folklore originating in a Greek myth*) a spirit living in trees or woods

dumbfounded *adj.* amazed; struck dumb with astonishment

duplicity *n.* deception; doubledealing

dwarf *n.* (*used in this story in the folklore sense*) a small, manlike, ugly creature with magical powers and often described as being good at mining for precious metals and gemstones

dynasty *n.* a sequence of hereditary rulers

earshot *n.* the distance within which sounds can be heard

earthenware *n.* pots or other containers made from baked clay

eavesdropping *v.* listening secretly to the conversations of others

eccentric *adj.* odd; unconventional

ecstatic *adj.* in a state of rapturous delight or joy

e.g. *abbrev. exempli gratia (Latin)* for example. Now often shortened to eg

elaborate *v. Chapter 5 (Jane)*: to give more detail in a story or account; to expand upon
adj. Chapters: 2 (Lackey); 5 (Wayne) and 13 (Petula Paucity): detailed; complex; complicated

elation *n.* extreme happiness; joy

electromagnetic radiation *n.* a range of energy emissions in a spectrum ranging from the longest radio waves to the shortest gamma radiation. Visible light is part of the spectrum

ellipse *n.* a flattened circle

elvensib *n.* see above in the *Animal and Elven Lexicon*

emanate (from) *v.* to come from

embellishment *n.* an improving detail or decoration; an adornment

embodiment *n.* an example of; a bodily representation of

emit *v.* to send out

emphasis *n.* giving particular weight, importance or significance to a statement

enigmatic *adj.* puzzling; mysterious

ensure *v.* to make sure; to guarantee

enthusiast *n.* one who is ardent or eager about a subject

envy *n.* wanting something belonging to another; jealousy; covetousness

epilogue *n.* a short piece of writing at the end of a story

erupt *v.* to burst out suddenly and forcefully

etc. *abbrev. et cetera (Latin)* and the rest; and so on; and the others

et seq. *abbrev. et sequens (Latin)* and the following. In the 'Notes on the names in the book' (above) it means that the name is not only found in the first chapter mentioned but also in other chapters that follow in the book.

exclude *v.* to keep out or leave out; to reject

excruciating *adj.* intensely painful; agonizing

exhilarating *adj.* exciting; stimulating in an enjoyable way

exploit *v.* to take advantage of another for one's own ends

exquisite *adj.* particularly beautiful; attractive with delicate or refined qualities

extant *adj.* still existing; still living; surviving

extermination *n.* complete destruction; annihilation; elimination; extinction

extinction *n.* complete eradication or destruction – especially of a species

extortion *n.* obtaining money by intimidation (frightening someone) or the threatening of violence

faerie *n.* a poetic alternative spelling to fairy

fairy *n.* (folklore) a small supernatural creature with magic powers. Usually portrayed as having diminutive human form

fait accompli *n.* (*French*) something already accomplished (done) and now unalterable

fanlight *n.* a small window above a door or larger window

fantasy *n.* a creation of the imagination

favouritism *n.* behaviour in which special attention or favours are given to a selected member or members of a group

feasible *adj.* possible

feint *v.* to make a misleading movement to deceive an opponent

feline *n.* (or felid) any member of the cat family, Felidae

felon *n.* one who commits a serious crime

FIFA *abbrev.* (*French*) Fédération Internationale de Football Association. The governing body of association football

figment *n.* an invention of the imagination; a fantastic notion; a made-up idea

financial *adj.* relating to money

fitful *adj.* occurring in irregular periods. A *fitful* sleep (Chapter 8) is broken and restless

flawless *adj.* without any defect or imperfection

fleck *n.* a very small amount; a speck

fleetingly *adv.* for a very short time; transiently; rapidly

flicker *n.* a brief, swift movement or event; a flutter

fluke *n.* something that happens by chance

flustered *adj.* in a state of nervous agitation; confused; upset

forensic *adj.* related to law. In Chapter 10 the police and vets are looking for evidence that might be used in legal proceedings against the 'petnappers' (qv)

forestall *v.* to anticipate something and prevent it

forty-forty-it *n.* see above in *Notes on the names in the book*

fraction *n.* a small portion of a greater amount or entity

fracture *n.* a break or crack. In Chapter 2 of a metallic component in an engine and in Chapter 3 of a bone

frazzled *adj.* (*slang*) exhausted; utterly weary

French window *n.* a long window, reaching to the floor, that opens like a door

frenzy *n.* wild excitement; frantic activity

frisson *n.* (*French*) a thrill; a shiver of excitement

frustrate *v.* to stop; to prevent; to hinder; to thwart; to annoy

furriclaws *n.* see above in the *Animal and Elven Lexicon*

furrow *n.* a groove; a trench; a wrinkle

gauge *v.* to assess; to estimate; to judge

genius *n.* one with exceptional ability or talent

gingerly *adv.* in a timid or cautious manner

glimpse *v.* to catch sight of briefly or incompletely

gnome *n.* (*folklore*) a legendary creature resembling a diminutive (small), misshapen, old man. In some folk traditions gnomes live mainly underground and guard underground treasure; in others they inhabit farms and houses where they may either help or hinder humans

goblin *n.* (*folklore*) a grotesque, dwarfish creature regarded as being malevolent towards humans. Goblins are greedy collectors of gold and precious stones

gormless *adj.* (*slang*) dull; stupid

gorse *n.* an evergreen thorny shrub with thick green spines

gossip *n.* idle chatter, often malicious; tittle-tattle

grand *n.* (*slang*) one thousand pounds

grill *v.* (*slang*) in Chapter 11 '*Grilling gorillas,*' this word is used in the informal sense of using prolonged or insistent questioning

grotesque *adj.* distorted; strange; outlandish in shape or appearance; bizarre

harmony *n.* agreement; accord

hectare *n.* a unit of area equivalent to 10,000 square metres or 2.471 acres

herald *v.* to usher in; to precede

heraldic *adj.* symbols and devices related to ancient families

hibernate *v.* to spend the winter in a state of dormancy

hitch *n.* a problem or obstacle; an impediment to a plan

hoard *n.* a store – especially of coins or treasure

hob *n.* (*folklore*) a diminutive (small) mythological creature with magical powers. Hobs are commonly thought of as household spirits. They may be helpful to humans but can be mischievous or malicious if offended

hobgoblin *n.* (*folklore*) a legendary mischievous creature sometimes called a countryside goblin. Puck, Shakespeare's sprite in '*A Midsummer Night's Dream*' is thought to have been a hobgoblin. In some traditions hobgoblins are Brownie-like creatures undertaking household chores and in others – as in this story – they are regarded as frightening and dangerous creatures

hominoid *adj.* manlike

hostage *n.* a person held captive in order to obtain a ransom (money) or the fulfilment of stated conditions

hover *v.* to remain suspended in the same position in the air by means of rapidly beating wings

humiliation *n.* a state of hurt dignity or pride

humungous *adj.* (*slang neologism*) very, very large; enormous

hysterical *adj.* in a highly emotional or excited state

i.e. *abbrev. id est* (*Latin*) that is; in other words. Now often shortened to ie, and often used incorrectly instead of e.g. (qv)

immaculate *adj.* without blemish; completely clean; unspotted

immortal *adj.* living forever; having perpetual life

imp *n.* a small devil or demonic sprite, often mischievous in nature

impassive *adj.* not revealing any emotion

impenetrable *adj.* something that it is not possible to get through or, as in Chapter 13, understand

imperceptible *adj.* too slight or subtle to be noticed

impish *adj.* mischievous

implicate *v.* to show to be involved

implications *pl.n.* effects or results that might not at first be obvious

import *n.* meaning; sense; significance

incognito *adj.* unknown; in disguise; under an assumed name or identity

incoherent *adj.* not making sense; unclear; distorted

243

incongruous *adj.* an unexpected or inappropriate mixture; unusual; bizarre; ill-matched; having disparate elements

inconsolable *adj.* incapable of being comforted

incriminate *v.* to suggest or prove someone's guilt

indispensable *adj.* essential; absolutely necessary

indulgence *n.* tolerance; liberal treatment

infamous *adj.* notorious

inferior *adj.* substandard; lower in quality or value

inset day *n.* an acronym for IN-SErvice Training day. A day when pupils do not go to school and teachers undergo training or fulfil administrative tasks

insurance policy *n.* a protection against a possible contingency

interject *v.* to throw in; to interrupt; to interpose abruptly

interquel *n.* (*slang neologism*) one of a series of stories that is inserted somewhere in the sequence but not at the beginning or the end

intervene *v.* to act so as to change the outcome; to interfere to change what happens; to modify or determine events

inverted commas *pl.n.* quotation marks. eg "example"

investment *n.* a deposit of money or other resource in a place or project where it will increase in value

involved *adj.* to be concerned with, engaged in, or implicated in some matter

iridescent *adj.* having colours that shine and flash and change with movement

irrespective *adj.* regardless of; not taking account of

irreverent *adj.* showing a lack of respect

irrevocable *adj.* unchangeable; unalterable

jargon *n.* specialized vocabulary or language associated with a particular profession or group

keel over *intrans.v.* to fall; to collapse suddenly or unexpectedly

ken *n.* range of knowledge

kettle of fish *n.* a situation or set of circumstances

kidnap *v.* to abduct someone and keep them captive

kinship *n.* relationship

K *n.* (*slang*) one thousand pounds

Krugerrand *n.* a South African investment coin containing 1 troy ounce of pure (24 carat) gold

league *n.* an old unit of distance equal to 3 miles (4.8 kilometres)

legend *n.* a traditional story from long ago that may or may not be true

lenient *adj.* tolerant; merciful

leprechaun *n.* (*folklore*) an elf-like magical creature said to be particularly associated with Ireland. A leprechaun is very mischievous and is usually thought to possess a crock of gold which it buries at the end of a rainbow

limousine *n.* a large, luxurious car which often (as in this story) has a glass partition between the driver and the passengers

logic *n.* reasoning; basis of argument

lore *n.* a collection of traditional knowledge or wisdom

lumberjack *n.* one who cuts down trees (*cf.* pollard)

malevolent *adj.* wishing evil on others, or appearing to do so

malignant *adj.* causing harm or evil

manipulate *v.* to handle or control, often skilfully

materialize *v.* to appear; to take shape; to become visible

mature *adj.* adult; grown-up; fully considered

mayhem *n.* violent confusion or destruction

mediocre *adj.* ordinary or average in quality

mellifluous *adj.* sweet; (literally honeyed); soothing

metabolism *n.* all the chemical processes that take place in a living organism

mimic *v.* to imitate or copy, especially for a comical or satirical effect

mock *v.* to ridicule; to treat with contempt or scorn

momentum *n.* the force of a moving object (in physics: the product of a body's mass and its velocity)

monetary *adj.* related to money

monitor *v.* to check on; to observe; to record

moon (time) *n.* a lunar month (i.e. 28 days, being the time from one full moon to the next)

mull over *v.* to think about slowly and carefully; to ponder; to study in detail

mute *adj.* soundless; silent

muted *adj.* subdued; restrained

mythical *adj.* fictitious; imaginary

mythological *adj.* see mythical

nail them *v.* (*slang*) to expose them; to pin them down; to incriminate them

napery *n.* table linen (tablecloth, napkins, etc.)

nefarious *adj.* wicked; evil

neologism *n.* a new word

nepotism *n.* giving favour to a relative or friend

neurosurgeon *n.* a surgeon who specialises in operating on the brain and nervous system

ninny *n.* a simpleton; a stupid person

nobble *v.* (*slang*) to injure or disable

non-negotiable *adj.* not open to argument or discussion; fixed

notorious *adj.* famous for something bad; infamous

notwithstanding *prep.* despite; in spite of

nugget *n.* a lump or small piece – especially of gold

nuts *adj.* (*slang*) insane; mad

nymph *n.* a mythological spirit of the fields and woods in the form of a beautiful maiden

oaf *n.* a stupid lout

oblivious *adj.* unaware (of); taking no notice

obscene *adj.* grossly indecent or immodest

offshore bank *n.* a bank located in a country with lenient tax laws

ominous *adj.* threatening; foreboding harm or evil

opal *n.* a gemstone found in igneous rocks

opalescent *adj.* having a milky iridescence similar to an opal (qv)

ore *n.* a mineral or mineral compound from which useful constituents such as metals can be extracted

ostensibly *adv.* seemingly; apparently

outmanoeuvre *v.* to gain an advantage by skilful moves or tactics

PA *abbrev.* personal assistant

pallid *adj.* lacking colour; drained of colour; pale

pang *n.* a sudden, sharp, brief sensation, usually unpleasant (such as of pain, emotion or hunger)

pan *v.* to manipulate a film or video camera so as to obtain a different view (e.g. close-up, panorama, etc.)

panther *n.* a leopard

paralyse *v.* to prevent from being able to move; to render immobile

pathological *adj.* (*slang sense in this story*) having a very strong compulsion or motivation

paucity *n.* dearth; insufficiency; fewness

penetrating *adj.* having the ability to pierce or enter

penthouse *n.* a flat built on the top of an apartment or office block. It usually has a good view and is often luxuriously furnished

perfunctory *adj.* cursory; superficial; without great attention

perplex *v.* to puzzle; to confuse; to bewilder

petnap *v.* a neologism (qv). It means to kidnap a pet rather than a person

petnapper *n.* a neologism (qv). One who kidnaps pets

phenomenon *n.* a remarkable occurrence or event

phoenix *n.* a large and colourful mythological bird that lives for a thousand years. It then sets fire to itself and from the ashes of this fire crawls a worm. In three days this grows into a new phoenix which then proceeds to repeat the cycle of life, death and regeneration

piece of cake *n.* (*slang*) easy; straightforward

Pit Bull terrier *n.* a fierce and aggressive breed of dog. It is illegal to own such a dog in the UK without a specific court exemption

pixie *n.* (*folklore*) an elf-like creature said to be particularly common in Cornwall and Devon. Pixies are kind to humans but very mischievous. They are child-like in nature and love to dance and wrestle.

pledge *n.* a promise or vow

Pleistocene *n.* the first epoch of the Quaternary period. It lasted from 1.8 million years ago to 10,000 years ago

plunder *v.* to steal by force

poacher *n.* one who hunts wildlife illegally

pollard *v.* to prune a tree in such a way as to stimulate bushy growth

ponder *v.* to think thoroughly and deeply about something; to give careful consideration to something

pooh-pooh *v.* to express scorn or disdain; to pour ridicule

posh *adj.* elegant; fashionable; smart; upper class; exclusive

postpone *v.* to put off until another time; to delay

posture *n.* stance; bodily position or shape; attitude

potentially *adv.* possibly

pouf (also spelt pouffe) *n.* a large, solid, cylindrical or cubic cushion which rests on the floor and serves as a seat or a foot-rest

preface *n.* a foreword; an introductory statement

preposterous *adj.* ridiculous; contrary to reason; absurd

prequel *n.* (*slang*) a story or a play that comes before another in the same series

pretext *n.* a pretence; a fictitious reason given to conceal the real purpose of an action

primate *n.* a mammal belonging to the order Primates which includes anthropoids and prosimians. Primates are characterized by advanced binocular vision, large brains and specialized digits for grasping

primrose *n.* a plant of the genus *Primula*. In folklore it is believed to confer invisibility on fairies and other magical beings

prodigious *adj.* very great; vast

prologue *n.* an introductory section to a story, play, speech, etc.

provenance *n.* place of origin

psychiatrist *n.* a doctor specialising in mental disorders

psychologist *n.* an expert in matters relating to the mind and mental processes

psychosis *n.* a serious mental disorder in which the affected person has a distorted sense of reality

PTA *abbrev.* Parent-Teacher Association

punter *n.* (*slang*) a customer or user

pyre *n.* a pile of combustible material (e.g. wood) to make a fire – especially for a cremation

quandary *n.* a puzzling situation; a predicament

qv *abbrev. quod vide* (*Latin*). This means 'which see' and is used to denote a cross-reference

racket *n.* an illegal enterprise

radiologist *n.* a doctor who specializes in interpreting images such as X-rays and body scans

rally *v.* to recover or return to order after a setback

ravenous *adj.* extremely hungry; famished; starving

recount *v.* to tell; to describe; to narrate

redress *v.* to put right; to correct; to make reparation for

reference *n.* a testimonial describing an individual's character, qualifications and expertise

reflect *v.* to think; to ponder

reflection *n.* careful thought or consideration

refurbish *v.* to restore; to renovate; to make clean and neat again

rejuvenate *v.* to make young again; to restore youth

remonstrate *v.* to protest; to point out errors

renovate *v.* to restore; to refurbish

resigned *adj.* accepting the situation; acquiescent; reconciled

retrieve *v.* to get something back

Rottweiler *n.* a breed of robust dog with a reputation for being fierce. Often used as a guard dog

rugged *adj.* uneven; jagged; rocky

ruthless *adj.* hardhearted; merciless

safari *n.* an expedition into the bush or wilderness, often in search of animals and especially in Africa

saga *n.* a story or series of events continuing over a long period

sarcastic *adj.* mocking; ironic; stating the opposite of what is really intended

satire *n.* scornful ridicule or irony

saunter *v.* to stroll at a leisurely pace

scam *n.* (*slang*) a swindle; a method of cheating

scan *n.* Chapter 3: a diagnostic medical imaging procedure

v. Chapter 14: to look rapidly over a large area

sceptic *n.* one who is doubtful or mistrustful

scrutiny *n.* close observation

sequel *n.* a story that continues a previously related narrative

sequence *n.* things happening one after the other; a succession of events

servile *adj.* fawning; obsequious

sett *n.* the underground den of a badger

shady *adj.* (*slang*) disreputable; of questionable legality or honesty

shaft *n.* a word or phrase that is directed like a missile

Sherlock *n.* Sherlock Holmes is the famous fictional detective in the books written by Sir Arthur Conan Doyle

short fuse *n.* (*slang*) a quick temper

shudder *v.* to shake violently in fear or horror

sidetrack *v.* to lead away from the main topic; to digress

signet ring *n.* a ring with a seal or family logo – originally used to authenticate letters or documents sealed with wax

sinister *adj.* threatening; suggestive of evil; ominous

slang *n.* a word or phrase that is not standard language but is used informally

sleek *adj.* smooth and glossy; shiny; polished

smarmy *adj.* (*slang*) unpleasantly fawning; flattering in an obsequious manner

smirk *n.* a smug, scornful smile

snigger *n.* a sly, mocking laugh – often partly concealed

snivel *v.* to whine in a tearful way; to sniff or snuffle in distress

solemn *n.* serious; formal

solution *n.* the answer to a problem

soothe *v.* to calm; to assuage; to make tranquil

Spanish Main *n.* the routes through the Caribbean Sea which were used by Spanish treasure galleons in colonial times and were a favourite haunt of English pirates

specific *adj.* relating to a particular thing; definite; explicit

spectator *n.* observer; onlooker; a person watching something

spectrum *n.* a range or scale

speculation *n.* theory; conjecture; supposition

spellbound *adj.* fascinated; enthralled

splice *v.* to join or connect – often in a seamless manner

splutter *v.* to speak in an incoherent manner – often with spitting or choking sounds

spontaneous *adj.* occurring naturally, without prompting or preparation

sprite *n.* (*folklore*) an elf-like creature, often associated with water

squash *n.* a fast, indoor racquet game using a small rubber ball

stable *adj.* steady; firm; balanced

stark *adj.* blunt; absolute; utter

static *n.* unwanted hissing and crackling sounds on a radio

stratagem *n.* a plan of action – often a trick or deception

stupefied *adj.* astounded; confused

stutter *v.* to speak with the constant repetition of some sounds; to speak hesitantly, haltingly, or with uncertainty; to stammer

subdued *adj.* unduly quiet; passive; cowed

surreal *adj.* having an unreal or dreamlike quality

surreptitiously *adv.* secretly; subtly; not in an obvious manner

suspended *adj.* temporarily debarred from duty or work

swirling *adj.* spinning; whirling; twisting

swivel *v.* to turn or twist. A *swivel chair* can turn on a vertical axle while remaining in the same position on the ground

syndicate *n.* a business group undertaking a project

synopsis *n.* a summary; a brief review

tactics *pl.n.* methods; plans; approaches

tamper *v.* to interfere or meddle with – usually for a bad purpose

taut *adj.* stretched tight; tense

tentatively *adv.* hesitantly; cautiously; uncertainly

tenterhooks *pl.n.* hooks used to stretch cloth. *On tenterhooks* means to be in a state of tension or anxiety or suspense

terminate *v.* to end

tetralogy *n.* a series of four related works

thistledown *n.* the feathery seeds of a thistle plant – well-known for being extremely light

thrash *v.* to beat hard. In the context of sport, a very convincing win

tick over *v.* to operate slowly. An engine 'ticking over' is running at its lowest rate, i.e. without any pressure on the accelerator

topic *n.* subject of conversation or interest

trajectory *n.* the path through the air or space of a moving object

transformer *n.* a device that changes the electrical voltage between circuits

transmogrify *v.* to transform into a different shape

transparently *adv.* obviously; clearly

traumatised *adj.* injured or wounded, physically or, as in Chapter 13, emotionally

treasure-trove *n.* treasure of unknown ownership discovered in a hiding place. It is the property of the Crown

trial *n.* a test or experiment

tribulation *n.* a cause of suffering or distress

trilby *n.* a felt hat with a brim and a dented top

trilogy *n.* a series of three related works

triumphal *adj.* celebrating a victory or triumph

troy *n.* a system of weights used to measure precious metals and gemstones (after the city of Troyes in France)

truculent *adj.* aggressive; obstreperous; argumentative; sullen

tumultuous *adj.* riotous; uproarious

turmoil *n.* confusion; tumult

twinkle *n.* a very short period of time; an instant

ultimate *adj.* final; last

unassailable *adj.* impregnable; able to withstand any attack

undeniable *adj.* impossible to prove wrong; irrefutable

undertake *v.* to promise to fulfil a task or mission; to commit oneself

unpredictable *adj.* changeable; capable of behaving in a surprising way

USB *abbrev.* Universal Serial Bus. A USB memory stick or flash drive is an electronic device for the storage and easy transport of large data sets. Now often in lower case: *viz.* usb

usher *v.* to show in or out; to escort

venomous *adj.* poisonous

vice *n.* an appliance for gripping objects very tightly

vigorously *adv.* energetically; robustly

villain *n.* a wicked person

VIP *abbrev.* Very Important Person

virtually *adv.* almost; practically; in effect; nearly

viz. *abbrev. videlicet* (*Latin*) namely; for example

vulnerable *adj.* capable of being hurt or wounded; weak

waveband *n.* a particular frequency or range of frequencies. Used especially in respect of radio transmissions

witticism *n.* a funny remark

woe *n.* a misfortune; a cause of distress

wrack *v.* to cause distress or suffering (also spelt *rack* in this meaning)

wraith *n.* a ghost or apparition; an entity lacking substance

wrench *v.* to give something a sudden or violent pull; to pull or twist forcefully

Unit Conversion Table

1 inch = 2.54 centimetres
1 foot = 12 inches = 0.3 metres
1 yard = 3 feet = 0.91 metres
1 mile = 1760 yards = 1.61 kilometres
1 league = 3 miles (*archaic*)
1 acre = 4840 square yards = 0.405 hectares
1 pound = 16 ounces = 0.45 kilograms
1 ton = 2240 pounds = 1016 kilograms

1 centimetre = 0.39 inches
1 metre = 3.28 feet = 1.09 yards
1 kilometre = 0.62 miles
1 hectare = 10,000 square metres = 2.471 acres
1 kilogram = 2.2 pounds
1 tonne (metric ton) = 1000 kilograms = 2204.6 pounds

About the Author

The author has had a distinguished career as a medical professor in which his publications, research and teaching established him as an eminent writer and international leader in his field. He was a pioneer in the development of methods of investigation and treatment that are now routinely used in medical practice and he played a major role in the introduction of computer technology into medicine. Using the pen name David Alric his writing experience and scientific knowledge have now been brought to a very different readership. In his first set of novels, *The Promised One, The Valley of the Ancients* and *African Pursuit*, he combined his storytelling skills – honed by years of reading to his children and grandchildren – with his interest in natural history and science to create a fascinating mixture of adventure, fantasy and fact. Now, in *Goals for Gold*, the author loses none of his magic in a gripping footballing tale which sees two schoolboy heroes pitted against clever and ruthless villains.

David has six grandchildren who are his most severe critics.